Precise Oaths

Paige E. Ewing

CITY OWL
PRESS

PRECISE OATHS
Liliana and the Fae of Fayetteville, Book 1

CITY OWL PRESS
www.cityowlpress.com

Cover Design by MiblArt. All stock photos licensed appropriately.

Edited by Lisa Green.

For information on subsidiary rights, please contact the publisher at info@cityowlpress.com.

Print Edition ISBN: 978-1-64898-385-6

Digital Edition ISBN: 978-1-64898-386-3

Printed in the United States of America

PRAISE FOR PAIGE E. EWING

"Paige Ewing has written a romp of a book in Precise Oaths. Liliana is an engaging, sympathetic heroine with a striking view of the world. One of the things I enjoyed was the way it made me look at being neurodivergent in a new way without once being preachy. What's more, Precise Oaths is tremendous fun. Liliana's quirky worldview is mixed with pure determination and ingenuity, along with a strong moral core. The writing is clean and flowing, with a host of terrific characters and great worldbuilding. It's hard to write a thought-provoking book that's also fun to read, but Paige pulled it off in spades." — *Angela Knight, New York Times Bestselling author*

"Liliana may not always know how to act with humans, but she has deep knowledge of the ways of the Fae and the Others. Some unlikely alliances and Liliana's abilities give us a rollicking adventure and set the stage for more stories to come. It's a lovely book and I look forward to reading the sequels. I need to know what happens next!" — *Nancy Jane Moore, author of The Weave*

To my mother, Janice Service, who helped build a love of books into my life from a young age, and told me, "You be what you want to be. I don't care if you want to dig ditches for a living. But if you want to dig ditches, then you better be the best damn ditch digger you can be." I'm writing books, but I swear, I'm the best damn book writer I can be.

Chapter 1

Madame Anna Sees All

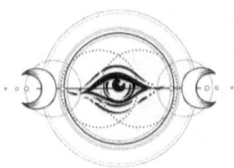

People who knew about Others thought spider-kin seers couldn't be surprised, but even Liliana could only see what she looked for. No one wakes up and wonders, *Will a Celtic werewolf accuse me of murder today?*

Liliana simply looked to see what the weather would be, just as she did every morning. When her fourth eyes showed her a fast-forward movie of clouds gathering and drizzly rain, she put on warm blue knit tights under her purple velvet skirt.

Her only plan for the day was to clean and organize before her favorite client's appointment. Janice Willoughby had been her client for over a decade. The room-bot that kept her floors spotless and dusted everything it could reach was a thank you gift from Mrs. Willoughby. Something to do with Liliana's advice helping her to become Mrs. Willoughby. She even invited Liliana to her wedding ten years ago in the Fayetteville Community Church.

The spider-kin seer didn't go of course. Weddings were filled with crowds of strangers. But it was still nice to be invited. And the room-bot was marvelously useful.

Unfortunately, the handy bot's telescoping arms couldn't reach to dust the highest shelves in the room where the spider seer conducted business. Liliana balanced on her ballet-slippered toes between the back slats of a wooden chair and the edge of a shelf while she dusted. Out of boredom, she let her fourth eyes wander. Large and cat-slanted, the eyes opened on her forehead above her eyebrows, lavender and teal opalescent colors swirling.

She saw three strangers on her front porch. The shortest one would knock on the front door—very soon by the sharp, barely future shading of the vision. She glanced at the nicely dressed short woman's wrist phone as she lifted her hand to knock.

She had only a minute or two until they arrived, depending on how accurate the time on the woman's wrist phone was.

Strangers.

Liliana twisted the dust rag in her hands. Strangers often laughed at her or spoke to her slowly as if she were stupid.

Her clients understood that Liliana had trouble sometimes remembering to follow social rules. Strangers expected her to already know and follow all the rules.

Who made up the social rules anyway? How does everyone else always know them?

She sighed in frustration, balanced on one toe tip on the chair's back for a moment, then hopped lightly down to the hardwood floor. She tossed her dust rag onto the corner shelf next to the pile of unfolded scarves.

There was no avoiding it. The three people did not look like they wanted her to convert to their religion or to sell her anything. She would have to answer the door.

Liliana closed all six of her inhuman eyes out of careful habit and brushed her thick, black hair forward with her fingers on both sides. Her hair would help obscure the tiny crinkles from closed spider eyes on her forehead and temples. Her appearance should now be indistinguishable from a young adult human. All three of Liliana's parents had worked hard to teach her how to blend around humans. Normals could sometimes be violently intolerant of those who were different, and Liliana didn't want to have to kill anyone today.

She cracked the door just as the short woman's knuckles were about to touch it. That let in the traffic noise of the busy street in front of her house.

The three strangers were taken aback for only a moment. Lots of people had door cameras these days and might have been warned by their house AIs watching through those mechanical eyes.

Maybe these people were driving by and saw my sign.

The big sign outside said, "Madame Anna Sees All." It wasn't true, since no one could see all without going insane, but her second mother urged her to paint it five decades ago. Ixchel said that advertising did not have to be accurate, only catchy.

Curiosity tickled the back of every part of Liliana's mind. Some part sent her a thrill of possible danger, but she couldn't trace it. Perhaps the warning was from a part of her mind that used one of her closed sets of eyes. She would check after her strange visitors left.

A brief glance with her first eyes, her dark blue human eyes, told her only one of the three people on her doorstep was a man. He wore jeans, an open synth-leather jacket, and a black T-shirt with white letters and a stick figure that said, "Stand back. I'm going to try...science." Disproportionately large, shiny black combat boots stuck out from his ordinary jeans.

She stared at them. He must have very big feet.

Those look like actual leather, made from cows.

Taxes on leather and other animal products had made them an expensive rarity since 2036, when the Green Party swept the elections toward the end of the Energy Wars.

The short woman in the blue synth-silk suit held up a shiny gold badge in the general direction of Liliana's wandering gaze. Her skin was perhaps the darkest shade Liliana had ever seen on a human, and she wore her hair in neat, shoulder-length braids. Her stature put her face nearly level with Liliana's. An agreeable coincidence. There were not many people as petite as she was.

Keeping her smile carefully small so her fangs wouldn't show, Liliana smiled at the woman's sensible but dressy flats.

"Good afternoon, ma'am. I'm Detective Shonda Jackson. This is the CID liaison with Fort Liberty, Sergeant Zoe Giovanni, and special CID consultant, Doctor Peter Teague." She indicated the other two people, who nodded in turn. "We'd like to ask you a few questions."

"Questions," Liliana repeated. The tightness in her shoulders relaxed. Everyone came to ask her questions. They must be new clients then. She waited for them to ask.

"Yes," the police detective confirmed.

Liliana considered opening her third set of eyes to look at these new people properly, but she couldn't risk her inhuman eyes being noticed. There were about a hundred Normals for every Other, so the likelihood was high that any new strangers she met were Normal.

The third stranger, a tall, pretty soldier with Army sergeant's stripes, looked at the sky. She had no makeup, an athletic build, and a pained expression.

Liliana looked at the sky too, but saw only the clouds and drizzle she had already seen with her fourth eyes that morning. There did not appear to be anything unusual up there.

"Ma'am, could we come in?" the soldier asked.

"Oh!" Clients asked questions at the table, not on the front steps. Liliana had forgotten to invite them in, and strict social rules prohibited them from entering without her permission.

The soldier's name was Zoe Giovanni, but her customers taught Liliana that social rules demanded she call soldiers by their rank and last name. She didn't know about civilian police officers, though, since she'd always avoided interactions with them. She assumed she should use the policewoman's rank, but should she use the detective's first name, Shonda, or her last name, Jackson? It was probably different from the military.

"Yes, Detective Shonda, Sergeant Giovanni, Doctor Teague. Please, come in." She opened her door wide, bowed gracefully, and gestured for the three strangers to enter her work space with her usual flourish of flowing sleeves. Dramatic motions were expected from seers.

"That's Detective *Jackson*." The short woman crossed her arms and pressed her lips together.

Liliana's cheeks heated. That had to be a new record, even for Liliana. It usually took more than a few seconds before she managed to annoy someone that much. "I am sorry, Detective Jackson."

She closed the door, muffling the traffic noises. The formal dining room Liliana had converted into her business was not ready to receive visitors. The pile of new, unfolded scarves lay messily on the shelf near the closed door to the rest of her house. The goddess symbols, crystals, and other arcane bric-a-brac on the higher shelves were still dusty. And the large crystal ball was off-center on the round table in the middle of the room.

Hastily, Liliana moved it two inches to the left.

The three people stood among her scarves and clocks and mystical knick-knacks peering around curiously, filling up a lot of space.

The spider-kin suppressed an instinctive urge to squash herself tiny in a corner of the room. "Sit down."

The strangers started at her abrupt order.

She winced at her own tone. She'd meant that to be an invitation but didn't get the voice inflection right.

To fix her social mistake, Liliana added a graceful gesture with one arm accented by the butterfly sleeves of her hibiscus-print silk blouse. She might not be good with her voice, but after growing up dancing on the high lines of a circus, no one could fault her physical grace.

They sat in the three client chairs around the far side of the round table.

Liliana chose a sheer, rose-printed scarf from a shelf and sat in the chair opposite the strangers. Now they wouldn't feel insulted because she didn't make eye contact. It was expected for her to stare at the crystal ball. She sighed with relief.

In the dramatic singsong that she'd memorized, Liliana said, "Madame Anna sees all. Pay me what you feel is fair for truth that cannot be seen by other eyes. I see what is, what has been, and what might be. Ask and the truth shall be yours."

She watched the strangers in the crystal reflections. Amused smiles played around their lips.

"Well, we did say we wanted to ask questions," Peter Teague said.

Sergeant Giovanni rolled her eyes.

Oh. They must expect a charlatan's show.

Liliana would have to prove to them that her sight was genuine before they would ask any questions of substance. She kept her smile small so as not to show fangs. They would learn what she could do. "Who chooses to be seen?"

Sergeant Giovanni grinned wide and shrugged. "I'll bite." She glanced at the detective for permission or confirmation.

Detective Jackson sighed, then nodded. "Fine." Liliana didn't know why the detective was still so annoyed. It seemed like a small mistake and Liliana had apologized. "I suppose we can start with that. It'll be interesting to see what the lady can do."

Liliana draped the scarf over her head as a veil to obscure her face. If they were Normals that didn't know about Others, she had to make sure they didn't notice when her inhuman eyes opened and closed. She waved dramatically over the crystal ball. When they looked at her gesturing hands, the spider-kin opened her third set of eyes just below the inner corners of her human eyes, like glossy black tears.

The sergeant's soul shimmered with color and energy, but not the distinctive, feral shine of a beast-kin, the cool green overlay of a plant Fae, or the hard edges of a mineral Fae.

A Normal. I was right.

Sergeant Giovanni's heart pulsed richly red, a passionate person, impulsive, someone who falls in love easily and deeply. Her inner self was riddled with the dark purple cracks of past heartbreak. A shell of pale yellow cynicism guarded her tender, wounded heart. "You have loved unwisely, Sergeant Giovanni. More than once, you chose forever, but forever didn't last."

The soldier with her long brown hair up in a neat twist at the top of her head arched an eyebrow. "Will I meet someone tall, dark, and handsome?"

Her cynical shell sought to hide the genuine question behind humor, but the answer mattered to the soldier. Liliana risked a quick peek with her fourth eyes, making an extra fluttering motion with her hands to distract the strangers.

Will Sergeant Giovanni meet someone tall, dark, and handsome?

Images solidified of a very tall man with strong, memorable features that Liliana found exceptionally handsome. Scars marred the smooth, dark brown skin on one side of his face. On one temple, a few strands of wiry gray mixed with black in a military short haircut. On the other, his ear was lost in scars, and a white streak marred the neat black hair. He wore a U.S. Army colonel's uniform, and he shook Sergeant Giovanni's hand in a vision with the only slightly faded shading of the recent past.

"A tall, handsome man with dark hair and skin and a burn scar on his face is already part of your life. He is someone you respect, an officer."

Liliana tilted her head, considering. This man intrigued her. The colonel's handsome face shimmered slightly, a sign that it hid something else, something Other.

What is he?

Some years in the past, he walked in a dry, barren land, armed and careful. Sergeant Zoe Giovanni followed, guarding his back.

"You follow where he leads."

A dying bush brushed the bare skin on the back of the colonel's hand. The bush bloomed.

Oh.

Liliana blinked her fourth eyes in shock. To affect plants so profoundly with an unintentional touch, the colonel must be Sidhe, the royal Fae who had the strongest ties to the Green. She hadn't thought there were any Sidhe on this continent, and yet, someone who obeyed a Sidhe sat across the table from her.

Her hands gesturing around the crystal ball faltered. Sidhe from the seelie day court were indirectly responsible for the near extinction of her species. She swallowed hard.

He is only a vision.

To keep from leaving a trail of blooming flowers and greening grass everywhere he went, a Fae with that level of power would have to suppress his aura constantly. That required an intense level of vigilant control.

Why does he hide his power?

Instead of looking for visions, Liliana thought about the veil over her head and the Normal woman with the passionate soul who sat across from her.

There are many good reasons to hide what you are.

For the merest moment, she considered telling Sergeant Giovanni what her tall, handsome colonel really was, but then winced at a scolding voice in her memory. "My daughter will be a woman of discretion, an *ehemythos*, not a tale-teller blaring the secrets of others as if she had the right." Her fourth eyes helpfully supplied a glimpse of her father's swarthy face, grim with anger.

"He has a will of iron," Liliana said carefully. That was probably not a secret.

DoctorTeague nudged the sergeant with an elbow. "You gotta admit, Zoe, 'a will of iron' fits Colonel Bennet to a tee, and he's tall, dark, and handsome with a burn scar on his face."

"Oh, you think the colonel's handsome, huh?" the sergeant teased. "Should I tell him about your crush? Should I warn Ben he's got competition?"

Liliana shuddered, only half listening. This powerful Fae colonel must live right on the Fort Liberty Army base, mere blocks from her house. The vividness of his face in her vision indicated a high probability she would encounter him in person in the near future.

More visions of Sergeant Giovanni and the dangerous Fae colonel flashed rapidly in Liliana's fourth vision. "You have served with him in many battles. He has killed to protect you, and you to protect him." *And in addition to possessing powerful magic, he is a formidable warrior.*

While the spider-kin hated even the idea of moving away from the clients she had guarded for years and her cozy home and routine, Seattle had the advantage of being on the other side of the continent from the Sidhe.

These people followed him. Perhaps that had been the hint of danger she sensed earlier?

Detective Jackson raised her eyebrows. "Is all that accurate?" she asked the other two.

"All true," the red-headed scientist confirmed.

The detective whistled low. "Impressive."

"Forget about it." Sergeant Giovanni waved a hand carelessly. "Anyone could listen to the scuttlebutt and know all kinds of things about our unit. Soldiers gossip like old ladies."

"There's one problem with your theory," Detective Jackson pointed out. "In order to brush up on you and your CO's past, Madame Anna would have had to know who was coming. I didn't call ahead. Did you?"

Uncertainty swept over Sergeant Giovanni's face. "It's some sort of trick." Her dark eyes narrowed in suspicion. "Aren't you supposed to tell me I'm going to meet the man of my dreams and live happily ever after?"

Liliana put aside persistent visions of the sergeant's dangerous commanding officer and peeked at her romantic future. What she saw made the spider-kin cringe. "You will meet a man soon who will give you chocolate and jewelry, but he is dishonest. He desires another." Sergeant Giovanni did not seem very skilled at choosing her mates. "Do not trust the man with the silver rose. Absolutely do not wear the locket."

The sergeant shook her head and laughed. "Seriously? You need to go back to fortune-teller school or whatever. That fortune sucks."

This objection Liliana had heard before. In her practiced singsong voice, she said, "I see only the truth of what might come to pass, not what you wish the truth to be."

"She's got you there," the detective said with a chuckle.

Liliana glanced with her third eyes quickly at the policewoman from under her veil. She saw grudging respect dawn in her sharp eyes, along with a firework sparkle of suppressed laughter.

The spider-kin smiled back. This police detective was also a Normal, with deep moral principles. The rich, dark blues of profound courage interlaced her aura, shaded generously with the softer green of compassion.

Detective Jackson's smiling eyes turned to a squint as she tried to see the spider seer's face better through the obscuring veil.

Quickly, Liliana closed her third eyes.

Peter Teague nudged Sergeant Giovanni with an elbow. "We didn't actually come here to talk about Zoe's terrible taste in men."

Sergeant Giovanni's wry face reflected in the crystal ball.

"You have questions. Now, ask and I will answer." Liliana waited patiently.

"Right," Peter Teague said, but he didn't ask her anything. The soldier and the man of science looked at one another, as if each expected the other to speak.

Detective Jackson rolled her eyes. Perhaps the annoyance she kept expressing was not Liliana's fault. "Ma'am, we're investigating a string of murders. Soldiers from Fort Liberty have gone missing. Some have been found dead. We thought you might be able to help us."

Liliana stood up so quickly she knocked over her chair. "NO!" She tore the veil off her head and faced the corner, turning her back to the strangers.

Her second set of eyes, the domed green eyes that shone like polished chrome on her temples, opened without conscious thought as they always did when Liliana felt threatened. They allowed her to see in nearly 360 degrees, although in spectrums different from her human vision.

The man slipped one hand into the sleeve of his jacket to the hilt of a knife. The two women both had guns.

Liliana knew better than to startle armed people. She knew

better. She shouldn't have done that. She wished these strangers would just go away.

The spider-kin picked up one of her new scarves from the messy pile on the corner shelf. "No one asks me to see murdered people. I don't want to see murdered people." Her nightmares were rich enough. "Please, don't ask me to see murdered people."

She ran the scarf through her fingers, facing the corner of the room next to the inner door that led to her living room. Burnout velvet cloth was her favorite. The sensation of silk then velvet trailing in patterns between her fingers always calmed her.

"It's all right," Detective Jackson said gently. "You don't have to look at the murdered soldiers." Her voice soothed like someone talking to a frightened child. "We just want to ask you a few questions. That's all."

Liliana swallowed and nodded at the corner. It was all right. She'd misunderstood. They wouldn't make her watch people be murdered. "Okay."

Talking to people with her back to them was a violation of a strict social rule both her mothers had ingrained in her. "Okay. You can ask." She took a deep breath to steady herself and turned around, still holding and staring down at the burnout velvet scarf in her hands. "But I won't look. Okay? I don't want to see murdered people."

Peter Teague followed the spider seer to the corner of the room.

Liliana tried to step back from him, but her heel touched the wall next to the door.

"Right." His voice wasn't gentle like Detective Jackson's. "Tell us where you were last night."

CHAPTER 2

OTHER NATURE

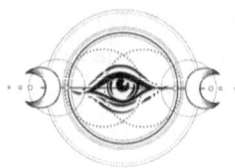

"DID YOU GO DANCING?" PETER TEAGUE ASKED.

Liliana smiled wistfully at the toes of his big combat boots. "I used to love to go dancing. I never liked the crowds, but the music was so beautiful. I would dance outside on the porches and balconies, and in the grass."

Their was so much music in her youth. People played instruments and swirled brightly colored skirts. Everyone danced in the evening after dinner for someone's wedding or birthday or just for the sheer joy of being alive. It had been so long since Liliana danced, she'd almost forgotten to miss it.

Peter Teague's brow wrinkled. "So, does that mean you went dancing or not?"

"There aren't any places to dance in the grass away from the crowds in Fayetteville. There's always too much noise and too many people, and the music is too loud. I don't go dancing anymore." It had been decades at least. She hadn't gone dancing in decades.

"Did you go to the Wolverines basketball game Friday night?" Peter Teague's voice had gained a more intense edge, but she didn't know why this scientist was so interested in what she did for fun.

"Go Wolverines," she muttered dutifully. It was socially required in Fayetteville to say those words whenever the local high school was mentioned. "I don't like basketball games at all. So many people screaming and shouting for nothing important." She shrugged. "And I always know who will win anyway. I never go to basketball games."

"Do you mind telling us where you were Friday night?" Detective Jackson asked.

"I was here. I have been rereading *Gulliver's Travels*." Liliana waved the scarf at the closed door beside her that led into the rest of her house.

"Is there anyone who could verify that?" Peter Teague asked. "Was someone with you?"

She shook her head. "Clients stay in the business space unless they have to go to the bathroom."

Liliana tilted her head to one side, puzzled by the seemingly random conversation. "Usually, when men ask about things like dancing and basketball games and my house, they want to have sex with me."

Doctor Peter Teague was attractive on the outside. If he was a nice person on the inside, she might enjoy having sex with him. She hadn't looked into him, though, so she didn't know if he was a good person, or even if he was human like the two women, or some kind of Other.

"Do you want to have sex with me, Doctor Teague?"

Doctor Teague cleared his throat and took a step back. "Uh, that's not um, I mean...uh, not that you're not pretty, but..."

Detective Jackson snorted.

Sergeant Giovanni laughed outright. "Give it up, Pete. There's no good answer to that one."

Liliana's ears flushed hot. When people laughed at her, it usually meant Liliana had missed something obvious to everyone else.

She replayed the conversation in her mind, trying to spot where her understanding had gone wrong.

Oh. Their questions weren't about Liliana. They were about murders. "Did the murders happen last night and last Friday night?"

"Ma'am, we're sorry we bothered you." Detective Jackson stood up. "We'll be going now."

"Okay," Liliana said, still confused. *Why did the detective not answer my question?*

"Not just yet," Doctor Teague said.

Detective Jackson's full lips tightened, and her eyes narrowed, making her look very fierce. "May I remind you this is my investigation?" She stood up and pointed at the sergeant and the scientist. "You two are only here in an advisory capacity, and so far your advice has led us on a big fat snipe hunt."

"I just have one more question," the red-haired man insisted, holding up a single finger.

Detective Jackson sighed and crossed her arms. "Fine." That looked like more annoyance, but definitely not at Liliana this time. "Ask. Then we leave this nice lady in peace."

Peter Teague turned back to the spider-kin. "Have you ever seen people killed by having their insides dissolved by acid and sucked out through two big holes in their throats?"

"Pete!" Sergeant Giovanni stood up and grabbed the man's arm, pulling him back from Liliana. "The lady is clearly..." She circled a finger around her ear. "...busy."

Liliana continued to look down at the scarf in her hand, so the soldier probably thought the spider-kin couldn't see, but Liliana always saw. "I am not crazy, Sergeant Giovanni. The word people sometimes use to describe me is 'autistic.' It's not really right either, but it's a better word than 'crazy.' I'm not crazy."

She forced herself to look at the soldier and the man directly for a second before her gaze dropped again. "Yes, I have heard of people killed in that way, Doctor Teague."

The two women stopped glaring at the man, and Sergeant Giovanni stopped trying to drag him out.

All three stared at the spider-kin seer.

Liliana swallowed hard. She hated when people stared at her like that.

Sure, she had seen that kind of death, but she certainly didn't want to see it again. It was a horrible way to die. Widow spider venom dissolved people while they were still alive.

Wait.

Widow spiders were spider-kin.

Every hair on her body stood on end.

Do they think I'm a widow spider?

Liliana rocked her weight onto the balls of her feet, her body ready in a moment to fight or run. She had seen enough of the detective and the sergeant's minds and hearts, she didn't want to hurt them. They were good people, but Liliana would not let anyone put her in a cage.

"Did you ask me those questions because you think I killed the soldiers?"

"You match the description of the woman we suspect, Madame Anna," Detective Jackson said, with an apology in her tone. Her arms were uncrossed, and she studied Liliana. It was the first time since she arrived that the detective showed no sign of annoyance.

The man with the big shoes shrugged off Sergeant Giovanni's grip.

His stare made her even more uncomfortable, like he was trying to tell her something, or ask her something, without words.

Was he some kind of Other?

Liliana put her hands over her face as if she were upset and peeked through her fingers at Peter Teague with the small, black third eyes by her tear ducts.

The man's pale, freckled appearance hid another face, a sharp-fanged canine face, and an intense aura of feral energy, like the scent of musk mixed with the color of lightning.

Wolf-kin. Though he looked different from other werewolves she had known. His aura was filled with more feral power. Most wolves were dark-haired and of Eastern European or Native American descent. She had only seen red wolves in visions and nightmares.

Peter Teague must be a Celtic wolf, one of the mercenaries who hunted down dangerous Others and killed them for money. Like the pack who killed her parents.

Terror hit her in the gut like a kick.

He was on the hunt for a spider-kin killer. Liliana was the only spider-kin in Fayetteville. His cold blue eyes watched her intently.

Ice water crawled over her skin.

Not this time. This time, I am not a powerless child.

Liliana threw her scarf in the werewolf's face and bolted through the door.

The wolf lunged for her.

She leapt over her couch.

His fingertips brushed her ankle, then his belly hit the wooden back of her couch. Air whoofed out as if he'd been punched.

Ha!

No one knew her house like she did, and no human or wolf was more agile than a spider-kin.

A pirouette on one toe spun her around the corner to her kitchen. She thumbed the switch on the room-bot. The waist-tall device with its long extendable arms trundled into the wolf's path.

Peter Teague tripped over her bot and face-planted on her tile kitchen floor. It sounded painful.

Liliana couldn't help but wince in sympathy as she slammed the back door shut behind her. It gave her a few precious seconds on her back porch, out of the wolf's sight.

In a swift, smooth motion like an Olympic gymnast, she leaped onto the railing around her back porch, caught the edge of the roof, and flipped her legs up. Her feet landed on the slanted roof.

Wolves hunt by scent.

She threw one of her ballet slippers onto the sidewalk and the other clear out to the quiet, drizzly neighborhood street.

Her body flattened against the wet shingles just as the werewolf pelted into her backyard. Her heart pounded so loud in her ears, she worried the red wolf would hear. She opened her fourth eyes so she could watch him without raising her head.

He found her shoe, then saw the other.

Take the bait, wolf. Come on. Take the bait.

Sergeant Giovanni ran out the door next. The werewolf raced off into Liliana's neighborhood, the human on his heels, rapidly leaving her little house behind.

Liliana smiled with fangs out.

You won't be killing a spider today, Celtic wolf.

Detective Jackson followed the other two onto the porch a few seconds later and closed the back door politely. The police officer watched the soldier and the wolf-kin scientist run up the street for a moment, shook her head, and muttered, "I still say it's a damn snipe hunt. If that lady knew anything about those dead soldiers before we arrived, then I'm the pope." At a steady jog, she followed the other two into the shady neighborhood.

Whatever a snipe was, Liliana felt some kinship with the creature in that moment.

She didn't twitch a single muscle until the detective jogged around a corner.

From perfect stillness to explosive motion, she skittered up her roof, leapt from the peak to the tall pine growing beside her house, then crept out onto the wiggly end of a high branch. With her wrist, she touched the rough bark. A dot of fluid from the tiny hole just below her palm stuck to the bark. As she pulled her hand back, a fine line of silk strong enough to hold several times her body weight formed where the fluid and air met.

The spider-kin looped the silk strand around the branch, drew an appropriate length out of the spinneret in her wrist, and scrambled down the line to the flat roof of the strip mall next door. She ran along the top of the long building, her feet clad only in knit tights, skimming lightly over the rough gravel roofs of the Troopers Army surplus store, the H&R Block, the barber shop, and the Virtual Fit net-based clothing store.

The roof was flat asphalt with gravel over it. Each rock jabbed her feet as she ran. A few spots of blood stayed behind as her wet tights ripped and shredded, leaving her feet bare on the rocks.

Thank goodness the red wolf was on the wrong scent, or he

would have been able to follow her blood trail easily. She ignored the pain and built up enough speed to leap clear across the narrow alley to the roof of Emerald Arms. That should break up her trail a bit, even if the wolf picked it up. She landed neatly on the foot-wide concrete ledge of the custom weapons store's roof and kept running. The concrete abraded the cuts on her feet, but at least it didn't add to them.

When she reached the end of the block, the spider-kin shimmied down a silk strand to the asphalt parking lot. She leaned against the brick wall, catching her breath and assessing her situation.

The old gas station across the street had been converted to a Starbucks when gasoline became obsolete in the '40s. With the entrance to Fort Liberty less than a block away, cameras hid everywhere. Camera drones circled overhead at periodic intervals. She had to move carefully to avoid them.

Liliana took her moment in a traffic lull to run across the street. She panted again, hidden under the cover of the Starbucks' green-roofed entryway, watching with her fourth eyes until the sky cleared of camera drones.

She ran some more.

Down Fillyaw Road, the shade of neighborhood trees gained density and became a narrow strip of true forest. Persimmon Creek ran through there, winding its way behind and between the neighborhoods full of houses for off-base soldiers and civilian contractors. The cradle of tall trees beside the creek hid her from curious eyes and airborne drone cameras.

The little creek had a grassy walking trail beside it. Liliana hissed in relief when her raw feet touched the sandy soil and green grass. She slowed to a rapid walk, probably far enough away from the werewolf that he wouldn't find her. She regretted sacrificing her shoes, but they had thrown the wolf off her scent admirably.

Liliana used her human eyes to see where she was going. Her fourth eyes opened to find out what the three people hunting her were doing. She kept her head down so her thick, black hair would hide the large lavender and teal eyes on her forehead if someone happened to look.

She focused on the red-haired wolf-kin with the blue eyes and the big boots. She needed to be careful with her attention split. It had taken Liliana decades to master her fourth eyes. Flashes of what might be and what had been could mix and wander through the visions of what was.

Her mastery of her most valuable and difficult gift was now to the point where she could perceive a double image, each sharp and distinct. It was as if she walked beside the creek far from the two humans and their hunting red wolf and beside them in her neighborhood at the same time. After decades of practice, her divided mind could now fully process those two sets of input and continue to do simple things like dusting or walking.

The three people quickly caught on that they had lost Liliana and stopped chasing randomly through her neighborhood. They returned to her house and took shelter from the chilly drizzle on her porch. Liliana hoped none of them would think to check the roof.

"Do you seriously think this Rain Man girl is our perp, Pete?" Sergeant Giovanni asked as they went up the wooden stairs onto Liliana's back porch.

The wolf-kin nodded. "She fits the description, and she doesn't have an alibi." Liliana noticed Peter Teague did not mention she was spider-kin, and the killer was almost certainly a widow spider based on his description of the manner of their deaths. Possibly his Normal companions did not know about Others.

Detective Jackson shook her head. "Maybe a hundred women in Fayetteville fit that description. Another hundred more if you include Liberty and the surrounding small towns." She rounded on the red-headed man, hands on her hips, and glared up at the taller wolf-kin. "Why are you so damn certain a mentally challenged fortune-teller, who doesn't seem inclined to swat a fly, is a serial killer?"

Peter Teague shrank under the short policewoman's glare. "She shares some other similarities to the killer...um...that I'm not at liberty to discuss, ma'am."

"Not at liberty to discuss?" The detective pointed a finger at the middle of the taller man's broad chest. "Well, I think you better get some liberty, Dr. Teague. This is a murder investigation, and if you don't come up with a damn good reason for me not to, I might decide to arrest you for obstructing it."

Sergeant Giovanni held up a hand in her friend's defense. "It's really nothing he can talk about, Detective. I'm sorry. You just don't have the clearance."

"Why is he even here? Just what kind of—" Detective Jackson made air quotes with her fingers. "—*special consultant* are you, Doctor Teague?"

"I'm an expert in um...biological anomalies?"

"Biological what?" Her eyebrows shot up. "Biological anomalies!" Detective Jackson took a deep breath and let it out in a relieved sigh. "Now I get why you two have been driving me nuts, speaking in half sentences since I met you. You are exactly the man I want to talk to. There are some things you just can't ask the forensics folks here in Fayetteville." She sat down in Liliana's cedar wood porch swing with the bright blue and green cushions. "So tell me, in your *expert* opinion, Dr. Teague, what sort of Other kills with acid venom like this?"

"You know about...uh...uh..." the wolf-kin stuttered.

"Others. I transferred here from N'Orleans. If you think the Other activity level around here is a little high, the Crescent City during Mardis Gras would have you crying to your momma."

Liliana nodded to herself. So, they were all three aware of the hidden peoples. Useful information.

Sergeant Giovanni held up a hand. "The United States government cannot officially confirm such creatures exist."

Detective Jackson waved that away. "I don't need official confirmation of diddly. What I need is a clue as to what I'm looking for." She rocked the porch swing in a slow glide. The height was just right for her. "I've been thinking maybe a Fae with toxic thorns, or maybe some kind of poisonous snake-kin, because of the huge puncture wounds, like fangs."

Peter Teague shook his head and sat down next to her. His knees poked up, but it didn't seem to bother him. "I thought the same thing at first, but not plant, and not snake. I analyzed the protein structure in the venom. Spider."

"Spider." Detective Jackson rocked and considered.

"Definitely spider. It has all seven of the black widow venom toxic protein structures, but with a much higher proportion of vertebrate neurotoxin and a completely unique organic acid."

"And why do you think Madame Anna is spider-kin?"

Peter Teague rocked with her, letting the detective's shorter legs set the pace. "She did a good magician's job of keeping us distracted when she was reading Zoe, but I spotted her opening two extra sets of eyes. My guess is she has another set I didn't see. Eight eyes. Spider-kin."

The spider-kin under discussion stubbed her bare toe on a tree root. The toe throbbed with far more pain than such a minor injury merited.

Why do stubbed toes sometimes hurt more than broken bones?

She added a bit more attention to her human eyes so she wouldn't trip again and berated herself for not being careful enough about hiding her spider eyes from the three strangers.

Back on Liliana's back porch, Detective Jackson nodded. "All right. I'll buy that. Having more kinds of vision would explain why she was the most precise and accurate fortune-teller I've ever met—and I've met a few in my day. She didn't use any of the usual vagueness, optimistic platitudes, or data fishing attempts, and she had no way to research our backgrounds before we arrived. But what brought us here in the first place? You two were awfully cagey about your reasons. I assume they're Other related?"

Sergeant Giovanni, who was leaning against the porch railing, crossed her arms and gave Peter Teague a pointed look.

His smile turned sheepish, and he rubbed the back of his neck.

"You know Siobhan, the little person who owns the custom weapons shop down the street, Emerald Arms?"

Detective Jackson nodded. "She modified my backup pistol. They don't make the grips with hands my size in mind."

"She's Fae and knows nearly every Other in North Carolina. She said Madame Anna was the only spider-kin in Fayetteville. Plus, Anna matched the description from the security cameras at the dance club and the witnesses at the game."

Liliana bared her fangs at the sandy path under her feet. Siobhan, the seelie Fae flower sprite, had put a mercenary on Liliana's trail. The spider-kin would not forget that betrayal.

"Dammit, Pete. I told you we shouldn't listen to Fayetteville's resident cuckoo cyber-fairy." Sergeant Giovanni sighed. "Your relationship with her is bad for your career and your mental health."

"Siobhan isn't crazy," Peter Teague hastened to reassure Detective Jackson. "She's just a little...obsessive." He turned back to the Army sergeant. "And Zoe, you shouldn't call her a fairy, at least not where she can hear you. The Fae consider that an insult."

"What's she going to do, take me out at the kneecaps?"

The red-headed man grimaced as if in pain. "Possibly with a machine pistol, yeah."

Sergeant Giovanni wrinkled her nose in distaste. "Even the supposedly sunshine and rainbow Others will stab you in the back. You need to spend less time with them, Pete. They'll warp your brain. They just don't think like people."

Detective Jackson raised an eyebrow at that, but she continued rocking without comment.

Liliana cocked her head to one side as she walked briskly, trying to ignore her tender feet. The sergeant did not seem to know Peter Teague was an Other himself, despite their friendship.

As Liliana followed the footpath into a larger patch of woods, she thought about leaving town, disappearing, and creating a new identity. She hadn't moved in five decades, not since her second mother died at the turn of the millennium. She liked Fayetteville. The weather was pleasant, and business was good. A constant stream of soldiers and soldiers' families, mostly Others, paid her to check on their loved ones as they fought far away. She even helped some Normal human civilians keep an eye out for whatever life might bring.

My clients.

Her steps faltered.

Moving would mean leaving her clients on their own. They would have no one to watch over them, no one to guide them away from danger and toward happiness.

She loved her job. It let her positively affect so many in Fayetteville, without forcing her into social interaction.

What would she do if she left? Join a circus again?

Her lip curled in an automatic sneer of distaste.

She had grown up in the circus, but she hated the chaos— always moving, always traveling. She liked the comfort of routine and stability. She liked her cozy little house in her cozy little neighborhood with her books and her pretty things.

A lot of circuses had gone virtual in the last few decades, traveling holographically rather than literally. That might not be quite as bad.

Liliana sighed and pulled the thin silk of her homemade blouse around her shoulders against the cold and drizzle. She was barefoot, her tights wet and torn, and she had no coat.

Before she could go someplace warm and dry and decide what to do with the rest of her life, she had to figure out what to do about the red wolf hunting her.

She tightened her fists.

Regardless of what her life would become, she would not die beneath red wolf fangs like so many of her kind.

The Fae colonel who paid the mercenary to hunt her needed to call him off.

CHAPTER 3

FAE COLONEL

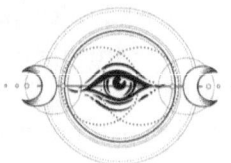

WITH HER FOURTH EYES, LILIANA SEARCHED FOR THE man who held the red wolf's leash. A Celtic wolf mercenary, once paid, would not leave the hunt unless his employer rescinded the order. She saw several images of the handsome colonel, but they were all on base. He lived in a house in Fort Liberty. He worked there. He ate there.

Liliana had lived for decades on the doorstep of America's oldest Army base. The huge base housed the third Army special forces group, Delta Force, some rumored special ops teams that no one was allowed to talk about, and a whole lot of regular soldiers.

Liliana had not received a Social Security number when she snuck into the country in 1943, stowed away in a cage full of lions, two of whom were her brothers. She had no driver's license and no chip ID embedded in her skin like many Americans born since the turn of the millennium. She did all her business in cash, or the modern equivalent, pay cards. She had a rule against her clients taking her picture. She did not appear on social media sites. Her business all came from word of mouth and a few who saw her sign. She avoided camera drones and CCTV cameras whenever possible. As far as the United States government was concerned, Liliana did not exist. The spider seer preferred for that to remain the case.

That made getting onto the military base very problematic.

Just when she'd begun to despair, and consider other options, she saw the Fae colonel leave base, today, just a few hours in the future, according to his wrist phone. He only drove a few blocks off base, on her street, to Emerald Arms custom weapons shop. He would park in the small lot behind the shop and go in to say something to Siobhan and come back out. After speaking to her, he would drive right back to base. Liliana had a narrow window to catch him.

While she could speak to him before he went in, she would have to be very careful. The colonel might be more dangerous than his mercenary.

She retraced some of her steps, keeping a close fourth eye on the Celtic werewolf and his companions to make certain they didn't return to the area. They went to the police station to research anything they could find out about Liliana on the computer.

Liliana chuckled to herself. *Good luck.*

When the colonel's car pulled into the parking lot behind Emerald Arms, Liliana would be standing in it. She sealed the back door shut with a spot of webbing so Siobhan would not interrupt them.

Under her skirt, she tied the equivalent of a climbing harness like the safety harness she used to wear in the circus. A line of her silk under tension led from just above the waistband of her skirt up to the roof of the building. In seconds, she could use that tension to propel herself onto the roof and get away.

She simultaneously needed to be close enough to the colonel to have a conversation and maintain enough distance to escape if he attacked. She should appear to him to be simply standing casually in the lot.

Plus, she knew better than to touch anything living when facing a dangerous Sidhe. Gravel and asphalt were the only things near her, unless she counted the stubborn dandelion growing in a crack a short distance from her foot.

She looked at it critically. The Fae probably couldn't use it against her. It was pretty, and she admired its determination. She left it alone.

Drizzle dripped down her face, annoying her as she waited.

At precisely the time she expected him, the colonel pulled into the parking lot and got out of his big, blocky, camouflage-painted car with the giant tires that looked like it could climb a mountain. It suited him.

"Hello," she said. He was even taller than he had seemed in her visions.

"Hello," he said, with a puzzled expression. "Do I know you?"

She hesitated for a moment. In her visions, she also had not noticed how nice his voice was, deep and smooth. It reminded her of Barry White. "We have never met, but I need to speak to you."

"I'm all ears." He gave her a broad smile that looked like he copied it from a magazine ad and a hands wide open gesture.

She looked at him with the only eyes she currently had open, her human eyes, unwilling to open any more in a parking lot in broad daylight. He did not appear to have any more than the one perfectly formed ear, since the other was lost in scar tissue. She didn't see any extra ears. "Um."

He chuckled a little. "I'm listening."

"Oh. Okay." Liliana spoke to the man's shiny brass belt buckle while scratching at the back of her neck where a drop of liquid managed to work its way through her thick hair to tickle her nape. "The last man I killed was over four decades ago. He tried to beat my elderly second mother and rob her. Before that, when I was much younger, I killed a man who tried to force me into sex, and one from a rival circus who tried to poison my little brother while he slept in lion form."

The tension changed in his body from relaxed to ready with only a slight shift of his weight to the balls of his feet. "Why are you telling me who you've killed?"

"I am not a murderer. I only kill when I must to protect myself or my family. I have not killed anyone in a long time."

His eyebrows went up. "Are you the one who killed my men?"

His eyes traced the path of a drop of water that ran around her eyebrow, down her cheek, over her jaw and neck, and down into her cleavage below the low neckline of her blouse. She became uncomfortably conscious of how the damp cold outlined her body and peaked her nipples.

"Your men?" she asked, shifting her gaze to his pseudo-suede combat booted toes so she wouldn't notice him noticing her so much.

"All the soldiers who've gone missing worked for me." He took a casual step closer to her as if to explain at a more conversational distance.

She couldn't take a step back without losing the tension that would let her spring to the roof rapidly. She held up a hand in a gesture for him to stay where he was. It was unlikely to be a coincidence for all the dead men to work for him. Their deaths were obviously also caused by a widow spider, and widow spiders only needed Other blood. "A lot of Others work for you." That was also unlikely to be a coincidence, since there were so many more Normals than Others.

"Yes," he said, his expression and lovely deep voice both neutral.

She nodded. So, he knew what his soldiers were. "Call off the Celtic wolf you paid to hunt me."

"I didn't pay him to hunt you."

Liliana blinked water off her human lashes, and even without her third eyes confirming his words, she believed him, at least the literal truth of his words. Sidhe were particular sometimes about their phrasing, but usually told the truth. So, this Fae colonel had not paid Doctor Peter Teague, and probably had not indicated that he should hunt her in particular. That didn't mean he hadn't asked the red wolf to stop his soldiers from getting killed, or that he would in any way discourage him now. She tried giving him back the same honesty. "I didn't kill your men."

He studied her for a moment, as if considering taking her word, then his fighting crouch became slightly more pronounced. "Teague and Giovanni are a sharp investigative team. I'm more inclined to believe them than a stranger, especially one accused of murder."

She sighed. This was getting her nowhere fast. He did not believe her, even though she believed him. Now he probably thought she'd killed his soldiers and only came here because he was next on her list. "Detective Shonda Jackson is also a smart investigator. She does not believe I killed your men."

"The civilian police detective assigned to the case?" He took a subtle step closer to her, making it look like a simple shift of weight from foot to foot. He was trying to creep close enough to grab her so he could use his superior size and strength to his advantage.

A good tactic.

Liliana nodded and sighed again. "You are not going to call off the red wolf, are you?"

"Not likely," he said, and there was something faintly apologetic in his tone.

She looked into his eyes, meeting them for just a moment. "I did not kill your men, and I intend you no harm either, if you let me be."

"I'd like to believe you," he said, and his voice softened. His face up close was compelling beyond anyone she'd ever met. Dark, smooth skin where it wasn't marred by a burn scar like a ripple in Damascus steel. High cheekbones, a broad nose over full lips, and a jaw so square, construction workers could use it to measure corners. His whole body stood solid, a pillar of determination and strength.

"I'd like for you to believe me too," she said. That moment seemed oddly suspended in time, as she met his eyes and a drop of water dripped from his hat.

She hurled herself toward him.

He brought his arms up to block an attack, but she wasn't attacking.

She landed in a crouch, her bare toes touching the asphalt for just a moment inside his reach if he hadn't been defending against her feint, and she bounced up as high as she could, using the rubberband-like pull of the line under extreme tension to add power to her leap. A high back flip in midair, and she landed perfectly on her toes, one hand on the concrete border wall of the flat roof of the building. "People who threaten me or mine die. Call him off."

The Fae colonel's jaw muscles jumped as his face hardened. He didn't have to say anything more.

She shook her head in frustration, turned, and ran. As she reached the end of the roof, she leaped over the next alley, popped out her arm blade, and cut the line. She took care to stay on concrete and asphalt until she was a good distance from the Sidhe.

Chapter 4

Wolf Trap

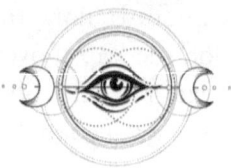

Setting a trap for the red wolf wasn't difficult. Once the trap was ready, though, she needed to find a way to draw the wolf into it.

Liliana looked with her fourth eyes into the high-end houses off Morganton Road on the edge of the little patch of woods across from the high school. One of them was empty, and the family forgot to set their electronic security system. Liliana entered through an unlocked second-floor window and borrowed their living room communication center. The five-foot, square holo-projector was able to pull in entertainment or social interactions from several hundred different satellite, internet, cable, or broadcast systems. It would more than suffice. She watched Sergeant Giovanni backward in time for a while until the sergeant called Peter Teague from her wrist phone. Once Liliana knew the red wolf's phone number, she touched the little picture that looked a lot like her old-fashioned house phone's receiver and pressed the numbers in the correct order on the screen. It took her a moment more to figure out nothing would happen until she pushed the green button labelled CALL.

"Hi, it's Pete. Who is this?"

A bigger than life holographic projection of the wolf-kin's head and broad shoulders appeared in the cube of empty space in front of Liliana's human eyes. "You are the Celtic wolf who seeks a spider-kin who murders soldiers." She watched the wolf in his van with her fourth eyes, a double image, matching the hologram in a way Liliana found fascinating.

Peter Teague sat in a vehicle cruising slowly down neighborhood streets on auto-drive. "Who is this?" he asked again, his brow furrowed in confusion. He frowned down at the dash where his holoscreen was blank.

Liliana had not kept up with the rapid progress of communication technology. She was not certain which of the many little images on the communication center's control screen would turn on the camera so a hologram of herself would appear in the wolf's van. "I am the woman you spoke to today. You asked me if I liked dancing or basketball games, and I thought you wanted to have sex with me. Face me as a wolf, and we will settle this. Do not bring either of the humans. I do not wish to harm them." A red wolf mercenary might not care if his human companions were endangered, but she did. "Come alone or I will disappear again."

She told him where to find her trap and hung up. She'd woven it in the forest near the shore of the little pond behind Westover High School.

Go Wolverines, she thought automatically.

By the time she returned to her trap, the sun had set, plunging the little patch of pine and oak forest into darkness. No moon shone that time of month, no streetlights were nearby, the clouds still blocked the stars, and the dense forest canopy cast the entire area into even deeper shadow. It plunged the little patch of forest into the near-total darkness rarely seen inside a city, an absence of light so complete, it rendered human eyesight useless. A Normal would not be able to see their own hand waving in front of their face. Even a wolf's sharp eyes would not help here.

Liliana climbed a tall pine tree in the exact center of the web and waited for her prey to arrive. She shivered. Her feet were like throbbing icicles against the rough bark, but at least the rain had stopped.

She tied back her thick hair with a strip of silk from the pocket of her skirt so she could keep watch better with her second set of eyes, the large, iridescent green eyes on her temples. With them, the details of the woods stood out as clear as daylight in all directions at once, but in strange colors. The nameless colors still made familiar things seem alien to her, even after using them for more than a hundred years.

While she waited and watched, a rabbit, in phantom shades that weren't actually red, crept out of its burrow under her tree. One long ear twitched and flicked as its tip encountered a trip line she had set. Each trip line was as visible to Liliana as if painted with glowing light, but invisible to anyone who didn't see in the same spectrums. Even the rabbit's sharp little button eyes couldn't see them. The dangling silk lines the spider-kin left hanging from dozens of branches glowed softly to show her the safe paths.

Her stomach rumbled, reminding her of all the silk she used. Enough time had passed since she laid the trap to replenish her web reserves, but she would need to eat the entire contents of her refrigerator when this was over.

As a matter of habit, the spider-kin attached a safety line to herself and the branch she sat on. Her first mother had drilled that into her. Solifu's voice, speaking precise French or English with her faint Egyptian accent, rang in her daughter's memory even decades after her death. "It never hurts to have a safety line, and it can often hurt a great deal not to have one." Liliana still thought of her first mother every time she set one.

I remember, Mut. I promise I will always remember.

She missed all three of her parents with a burning ache. They had been dead a long time, but when things went wrong, their absence hurt as deeply as a fresh wound. They had been a happy, loving triad. She'd never felt alone when they were alive, even at the lowest points of her childhood.

When she first opened her fourth set of eyes on her thirtieth birthday, Liliana had been flooded with so many maddening, unrelenting images of everything at once, she'd gotten lost. She'd withdrawn so far into herself, her parents had to feed her and dress her for a few years, as if she were a helpless baby.

Eventually, Liliana's mind found ways to cope with her fourth vision, dividing her consciousness and improving her ability to focus, shutting out what she didn't need to see. Unlike some other spider seers, she had never completely lost her hold on sanity. Some people thought she was insane, but Liliana wasn't. She knew this for certain. Before she died, Ixchel, her second mother, reassured her again and again. Liliana's problems were normal for an adolescent spider seer adjusting to her fourth sight. She trusted her second mother's judgment completely. If Ixchel said she was not insane, then Liliana was *not insane*.

Liliana wasn't a murderer either. She hadn't killed anyone in decades. The Fae colonel had no reason to send a Celtic wolf to hunt her.

She would have to convince the wolf-kin of that. Or more likely, she would have to kill him. A red wolf hired to kill was as unlikely to listen to reason as his employer had been.

With her fourth eyes, Liliana watched the red wolf, making certain he did, in fact, come alone. If he had a pack accompanying him, then she would run. One red wolf she could probably defeat, but Liliana did not like her chances against a pack. Even her father and first mother fighting side by side had fallen to a Celtic wolf pack.

The red wolf was no longer with Zoe Giovanni and Shonda Jackson. He had been auto-driving around the spider-kin's neighborhood in a big green van while he sniffed the air through the open window to pick up her scent. After her call, he drove to the apartment complex on Grande Oaks. He parked in front of the closed information center, under some trees where his van would be all but invisible from the street and passing camera drones. The spot would be unpopular since, in the daytime, it would not allow the solar panels on the car's roof to recharge.

His choice of parking place made it clear he did not intend for anyone to know he'd been there. That made sense if his intention was to kill Liliana. It would not do for a U.S. Army Criminal Investigation Division consultant to be seen parked at the scene of her murder.

He opened the back of his van, which was furnished like a tiny camper. He lifted a small couch with one hand until it clicked against the ceiling and stayed. He touched a spot on the van wall, and the hologram of carpet underneath disappeared. It revealed a hidden compartment big enough to hide a body containing things that made her shudder: an amazing array of knives, strange vials of colored liquids, and grenades. She even saw a rocket launcher.

The red wolf pulled out a battered old sword in a worn leather scabbard and strapped the belt around his waist. He stripped off his synth-leather jacket and put on a shoulder holster with a pistol. Extra clips went into the pockets of the jacket before he put it back on. He lifted his pant legs and strapped more knife sheathes to his calves, adding them to the knives already strapped to his wrists. A machete slid into a sheath behind his neck where the hilt barely poked above his collar. He tucked something that looked like a modified Taser under his belt in the back.

Liliana shivered harder, not just from the cold. She almost reconsidered her plan to fight the werewolf for her right to remain in her chosen home.

But she was trained for this.

Liliana's father and both her mothers had been fierce warriors. They taught the young spider-kin to fight from the time her arm blades first extended when she was five.

All three of her parents used combat practice to help ground Liliana back in reality when her mind got lost in various new kinds of sight. She remembered the feel of a weapon in her hand or her own natural weapons extended from her arms. She remembered the warmth of the loving hands of her mothers and her father, each guiding her in the practiced motions of different fighting styles, grounding her when her mind threatened to break. Liliana never had any desire to hurt others, but combat was natural to her.

Combat was home.

Liliana extended razor-sharp, slightly curved bone blades over a foot long from nearly invisible natural pockets in her forearms. She carefully measured a silken cord out, exactly enough to let her swing just above her trip lines, and crouched on her cold, sore toes, waiting for her enemy to enter the trap. Her hands trembled as she cut her safety line with her arm blade and measured out that final strand.

She tilted her head. The feeling was similar to what she felt before shows as a young performer in the circus. She could focus on the performance when she was dancing in the air on high wires or trapeze swings or silk streamers, but this feeling was a lot like looking out at hundreds of people waiting to stare at her.

Fear was not a feeling she experienced often. Not this kind of fear anyway—fear for her life.

Fear of being stared at or laughed at. Fear of crowds. Fear of stumbling through awkward social situations like a blind child in a forest filled with bear traps. That kind of fear she was used to. But fear she might soon die? She hadn't felt that in a long time.

She wished she could fight with her fourth eyes open as her first mother could, to see and anticipate enemy movements. Liliana's fourth eyes were more likely to distract her in combat than to aid her.

Below, the rabbit stopped nibbling greenery and popped up on its hind legs, long ears in the air swiveling for better reception. A moment later, the little animal vanished back into its safe burrow under the tree.

Liliana wished she had that option. She wished the handsome Fae colonel had believed her.

Her mothers would be so proud of her, though, for facing her fear and standing up to the red wolf. She blinked tears from her human eyes.

Her father would have been disappointed in her if she did anything else.

Liliana lifted her chin.

The quiver in her belly was just the echo of childhood nightmares. She was an adult now, or close enough. She would face the terror of her childhood and win.

Her hand tightened on the fine silk line to still the tremble.

Still in human form, the red-haired werewolf crept through the woods, making barely enough noise in the wet pine needles and sandy soil to alert the rabbit's keen ears. His gun was out; a bright compact LED light shone from the tip of the barrel. He held a knife poised, ready to throw in his other hand. The sword hung in the scabbard at his hip.

Peter Teague wasn't a big man in human form. He didn't look like one of the world's deadliest beast-kin, but his movements showed the grace of a natural predator. The bright beam of white light searched the forest, joined with the barrel of his gun. If the Celtic wolf caught so much as a glimpse of her, Liliana would die.

She could do this. The spider seer took a deep, quiet, steadying breath.

The red wolf muttered softly to himself as he stalked further into the inky shadows under the tall pines and oaks. "Walk into my parlor, said the spider to the fly."

Liliana smothered a surprised urge to laugh. She always liked that quote. Her head tilted to one side.

Was Peter Teague afraid too?

For the first time, she considered the situation from his side. Alone. He had no pack backing him. He clearly knew this was a trap, and he believed she'd killed several soldiers in a horrible way.

Yet he still came.

He sought to stop a murderer, and knowingly risked becoming the next victim to do it. No one paid him,. His own need to protect innocent lives drove him. Her father would have admired such a man.

The light on the wolf's gun barely scratched a tiny hole in the clinging blackness of the forest. He was all alone in the dark.

"Anna? Are you here?" Peter Teague called to her. "Anna, come on out and let's talk about this." He stepped deeper and deeper into the trap. She'd left some clear paths into the web, and he'd found one.

Her enemy was walking right into her trap all but blind. And she was a spider seer.

She could do this.

But maybe she could do it without killing the brave red wolf.

CHAPTER 5

AERIAL BATTLE

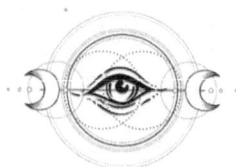

LILIANA SWUNG DOWN ON HER SILK LINE, SWOOPING AT him out of the darkness with her right forearm blade extended. First, she had to blind the wolf-kin completely and make sure he didn't shoot her.

She caught both his hands with the blunt side of her arm blade. She could have taken his hands off at the wrists with the sharp edge and ended their fight very quickly, but she chose a riskier path that might not end in anyone's death.

The werewolf's gun and knife flew out of his hands. The light didn't go out. The gun tumbled across the pine needle–strewn ground and came to rest behind a root, making an island of white light in her second eyes' ocean of nameless colors.

Peter Teague shook his hand where she'd probably bruised it. "Anna, we don't have to do it this way." The wolf-kin drew his sword. He pulled out another of his many knives with the other hand. "Just come with me, quietly. No one has to die tonight." His footsteps were grounded and careful.

She could tell by the way he kept his feet low that he was unaware of the trip lines. He was also nowhere near them. She sprang the trap too soon. He still had several steps to go before he hit the web.

Nerves.

It was too late to correct her mistake.

Liliana jumped off a limb and caught another dangling silk cord, kicking her feet to swing faster in a long, graceful arc.

She had missed this feeling of freedom as the cold night air whooshed through her hair. It felt like flying. Just as it had back in the circus when she performed, exhilaration overwhelmed fear.

She extended her bare feet in front of her as she swung toward him, intending to knock the wolf down and hopefully cause him to lose another weapon.

The wolf must have smelled her, or heard her skirt flapping in the wind. He sidestepped and struck out with his sword.

Desperately, Liliana arched back as the sword blade swished over her body close enough for her to feel the air move in its wake. The heavy steel blade twanged against her silk line, parting it barely above her fingers.

As her line jerked, then went slack, Liliana twisted and managed to land on her sore feet. Her heart pounded in her throat. Even virtually blind in the dense forest on an overcast night, the werewolf came within inches of killing her.

The wolf-kin spun to face her general direction, sword and long knife held at the ready.

Liliana swallowed. She breathed deep and slow to steady her racing heart and keep from giving her position away.

He clearly couldn't see her, but his head tilted slightly as he listened, waiting for her to move or breathe too loudly. He sniffed the air.

She had been all over this area setting her trap. Hopefully, that would confuse his sharp nose.

As silently as she could on her icy, sore feet, Liliana moved. The pine needles, cones, tree roots, and rocks made her steps tentative and painful. It was probably a good thing her kind weren't prone to tetanus. She hopped up delicately onto one of her low lines to get above the forest floor, wishing she hadn't left quite so much clear space between the trip lines. The familiar feel of her silk under the soles of her feet soothed them. Her steps steadied on the fine thread.

"Anna, it doesn't have to be this way," the red wolf said. "I just want to ask you a few questions."

"I do not wish to answer your questions. Not as long as you ask with blades in your hands."

The wolf oriented on her voice and shuffled blindly toward her, sword held high, long knife gripped like a second shorter sword in the other hand.

She bounced on the taut silk line under her toes, sprang up, and caught one of dozens of dangling lines. She scrambled hand over hand as quickly as she could. Just as the wolf passed beneath her, Liliana lifted her feet.

He held one hand out in front of him, searching for her by touch as he passed less than a foot beneath her.

That should lure him well into the web. Now, to close the trap.

Liliana dropped behind him after he passed, but she landed on a small twig. It snapped under her weight.

In a panic, she dropped flat to the ground as the wolf spun around.

His sword sliced the air blindly where she had been a moment before.

As silently as she could, she rolled to the side under two low lines, heart pounding. Pine needles stuck in her hair and clothes.

The wolf moved toward the sound of the twig, swinging the sword wildly in the dark. The blade severed a pencil-thin pine branch that dropped on Liliana's shoulder.

She twitched involuntarily, and the wolf's blade swung toward her. The wolf-kin might be unable to see in the dense shadow, but he followed every whisper of sound.

Liliana smiled with fangs exposed.

I can work with that.

The spider-kin kicked a pinecone so it made a skittery sound across the ground.

Peter Teague lunged toward the sound, swinging the sword blindly. The sticky silk of a trip line caught his ankle.

Finally.

The wolf sprawled full length on the ground. He lost his long knife but managed to keep hold of his sword. He braced himself up on one elbow, swung the sword down to sever the trip line tangling his ankle, then sat up.

He tilted his head, listening.

Liliana held her breath.

Thunk. Thunk. Two throwing knives embedded themselves in the trunk of the tree beside her. Liliana didn't even flinch. He missed her by feet. He had only the vaguest clue of her location.

As he regained his feet, she knew what she had to do.

She did a low plié in close to him, reached out, and tapped her wrist lightly to the back of the wolf's sword hand, attaching a line. He felt the touch and slashed over her with his sword. She dove over a trip line and under his swing, threading the narrow space, then somersaulted back to her feet and yanked him off-balance.

As the wolf staggered toward her, he used his momentum to shift the movement into a charge, arms held out wide to catch her. He growled low.

A werewolf didn't need weapons to be deadly.

He shifted to big demi-wolf form with long, clawed fingers. Fangs pushed out of his elongated mouth. His collar-length hair turned shaggy and thick and crawled over his exposed skin.

Liliana kept her hold on the line attached to his wrist, while she leaped upward and tucked into a forward flip. The wolf stumbled under her, right into her trip lines, but stayed stubbornly on his combat-booted feet. His boots no longer looked too big on the massive wolfman.

As he chased the phantom of another tossed pinecone, the spider-kin touched his other arm with a spinneret. When he tripped again, she tossed a few loops of sticky, fresh silk at him while he was on the ground, entangling him.

The wolf growled and struggled back to his feet, trying to cut her silk cords with his claws and yet another knife.

She misdirected and tangled him some more. She pulled on his limbs like a puppet master and flowed with his swings and steps as if he were leading her in a dance. Rather than fighting his great strength, she used it against him.

Soon, she got his sword arm wrapped painfully behind him. The other arm she pinned across his belly. Liliana took a deadly risk, darted in close, and attached the other end of one line to his sturdy, braided nylon belt so his arm was anchored behind him to his own body. He couldn't use the sword at all now.

A ghost of warm breath touched her throat as sharp fangs snapped at her. Liliana yelped in terror and jumped aside barely in time.

The wolf used that moment of fear to free the arm that wasn't fully anchored yet. Their battle had taken them near the trunk of one of the tall, straight pine trees. The wolf swiped at her with his claws.

Liliana dove behind the tree.

Claws ripped bark instead of her skin, spraying splinters of wood into the night rather than blood.

Holding tight to the line attached to his wrist, she yanked with all her might, the full weight of her body thrown into it.

The werewolf's own momentum helped spin him until his back slammed into the tree.

Behind the trunk, she pulled the line taut and touched both the line and a sticky spinneret to his shoulder on the other side of the trunk. His free arm was no longer free, but bent awkwardly behind the trunk. He yanked with all his great strength and only pulled his own shoulder tighter against the rough bark.

His strength fought itself.

Liliana kicked his hand to make him drop the knife.

She cut the top of her foot on one of his claws, but the knife dropped to the ground.

While he growled in a frustrated frenzy and tried to get his teeth on the cord holding him, she ran around the tree like it was a maypole, attaching as many lines as she could to him and to the tree trunk. He lost his grip on the sword as he struggled to angle the blade so it could cut her silk.

Ducking in, she snatched his sword away.

She couldn't get to his knives to take them away with her lines wrapped so tightly around him, but he couldn't reach them either.

The wolf snapped at her with sharp teeth and tried to trip her with his legs.

She'd immobilized his arms, but he was still dangerous.

He managed to cut a few strands with his claws and chewed through another with his teeth.

Liliana wound him round and round with more and more silk, securing his throat to the tree to hold back his vicious teeth, securing his legs to keep him from kicking or tripping her.

While he struggled and fought, she kept running around him, lunging in, attaching lines and dodging back out and around in a dangerous ballet. She added a half-dozen silken cords for every one he managed to break.

Soon, the red wolf could barely move. He could no longer reach the silk bonds with his teeth. She closed in behind him to bind his wrists with extra lines to immobilize his clawed hands completely so he could not twist up to reach the knives in his sleeves. She got close enough she could feel the vibration of his enraged growls and the surprisingly soft texture of his fur, damp with sweat. The distinctive odor of wet canine tickled her nose.

He shifted back to human form as a last resort. That loosened the coils of silk as he no doubt intended, but he was already too tangled to get away before she wrapped him round and round again tighter than before. With the tighter binding, he could no longer take the larger demi-wolf form or the differently shaped full canine form without strangling or cutting himself with the fine, tough silk.

There was no way he could get loose.

Liliana finally stopped. She panted with exertion and

adrenaline. The wolf-kin was bound securely. Very securely. She might have overdone it just a bit.

He couldn't hurt her now.

Fear still hammered in her heart, but to that was added a thrill of triumph.

I defeated a Celtic wolf.

She fetched his gun and dug its butt end into the sandy dirt and pine needles, standing it up to form a pool of white light around the two of them. She wanted her enemy to see the hundred-pound spider-kin who defeated the big bad wolf.

This deadly threat, this nightmare being that haunted her most terrifying dreams with the blood of her family dripping from his fangs, stood helpless before her, panting and rumbling his rage.

Now, the question was, what would she do with him?

CHAPTER 6

TIGER BY THE TAIL

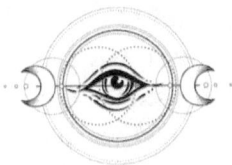

LILIANA SMILED FIERCELY, SHOWING THE WOLF-KIN HER fangs. They might be smaller than his, but they were needle sharp. She looked way up and met his eyes for a moment in challenge.

Her stomach growled loudly with hunger as the adrenaline rush began to wear off.

That was not helpful. How am I supposed to be intimidating with my limbs shaking and my tummy rumbling?

The trapped wolf-kin struggled frantically against the web, panting puffs of fog, white showing around his blue eyes.

Well, he does seem intimidated.

His human face with its cute, freckled nose made him seem young. She didn't believe he had yet seen thirty years. She opened her third eyes so he could not lie to her, and she saw the sickly green color of terror shading his inner self.

The wolf's fear pleased her and disturbed her at the same time. Uncomfortably, she dropped her human eyes to the pulse pounding in his throat but kept her third eyes open. She needed to see the truth of him.

Peter Teague stilled when it was clear he couldn't get free. "Anna, let me go." His calm, reasonable voice betrayed none of the fear making his pulse race.

Lillian scoffed. "I am not stupid, and I am *not crazy!*" Her voice shook as she gritted out the words. Between hunger and cold and the aftermath of combat, Liliana's hands were far from the only thing trembling, but she faced her enemy defiantly. "If I let you go, I know you will still try to kill me." Her hands clenched in angry fists.

Does he think I'm stupid?

"I just want to talk to you." His breath fogged in the column of light from the LED on his gun. His deep voice sounded soothing, like she was a wild animal he tried to calm.

Pride and anger straightened her spine to her full height, about even with the wolf's shoulder. "Fine. Talk to me then, Celtic wolf. Talk to me without your weapons or your fangs."

"Did you kill those soldiers?" he asked her.

"No. I did not." She forced herself to meet his eyes again. If she could make him believe her, then they could both go home.

"Then why did you run? Why did you set a trap for me?"

Her shoulders sagged. "I knew you wouldn't believe me. I know what you are. The colonel who owns your allegiance sent you to kill the murderer. You would not take my word over your employer's. And he did not believe me either."

He clenched his teeth. "No one sent me, and no one paid me. I'm no mercenary." His mind filled with images reminding Liliana of her nightmares. Red wolf mercenary packs slaughtering Others without mercy. His memories came from snippets of old combat footage. His horror at those images came close to the intensity of her own, and she had lived it.

She feared the monsters.

Peter Teague feared becoming a monster.

That surprised her. She looked deeper into him, curious about a red wolf who refused to kill for money. She saw unshaded honesty. He genuinely believed what he said.

Yet he clearly worked for the powerful Sidhe colonel, even if the Fae insisted he wasn't paying the Celtic wolf to hunt her. The wolf-kin thought he was there simply to stop more soldiers from dying, but Liliana's eyes showed her clearly the handsome colonel telling him and Sergeant Zoe Giovanni about the problem. He didn't promise Peter Teague money, but he did ask them to stop whoever was killing his men.

"You think I am a widow spider." Liliana shrugged. Even if the red wolf only sought to protect innocents, he still wanted her dead. "You would have killed me if I hadn't run."

"What's a widow spider?"

Liliana tilted her head. "Has no one taught you about the drinkers of life?" Vast knowledge of Others was passed down in the Celtic wolf packs. The wolves knew the secrets of the Others, their habits and weaknesses. That knowledge, carefully guarded by the red wolf packs, was part of what made them such valuable mercenaries.

He shook his head. "My mother and father were killed by unseelie Fae when I was little, and they were the last of our pack. I was adopted and raised by a human woman who didn't know anything about Others."

"Oh." Liliana felt oddly sad for the orphaned wolf, raised with no knowledge of his heritage. "I, too, was raised by a second mother who was not of my species after my other two parents were killed."

"I'm sorry." His face and voice sounded sincere. But he was certain she'd murdered soldiers and would murder more if he didn't stop her. He was still determined to get free and either kill her or take her to Detective Jackson to put in a cage.

Liliana could not let herself like this wolf. He was her enemy. It wouldn't hurt to educate him though. "When a widow spider is pregnant, she must inject into male Others acidic venom that slowly dissolves bones and organs while maintaining life as long as possible. Then, she drinks the men's dissolved insides while they're still alive. If the pregnant widow spider does not do this, she and many of her unborn babies will die."

"And you're not pregnant?"

Liliana ducked her head, embarrassed. She was not old enough yet to be pregnant, not for four more years when she reached her one hundred fiftieth birthday. But she did not have to tell her enemy that. "I am not a widow spider. Just as you are a Celtic wolf, not an ordinary wolf-kin. I am a different kind of spider-kin, a spider seer." Liliana opened all her eyes at once and showed him.

"Whoa." The wolf looked at her face with wonder even in the midst of his fear. "I just saw glimpses of your eyes this morning, behind the veil. I didn't get a chance to really look at them."

As the wolf admired her eyes, she looked deeper into him with all her eyes at once. She sought not just to know if he spoke truth or lies, but who he truly was inside.

First, his high intelligence was obvious. His mind churned through possibilities and probabilities based on the evidence he'd seen. Images of the gruesome murders flashed past. A woman about her height and build had been caught on a poor resolution security camera at the night club and described by witnesses at the basketball game. Street and drone cameras had not been able to track where she took the men. They were found later, dead in hotel rooms.

His suspicious, calculating mind was exactly what she would expect from someone who worked as a scientific consultant with the military police.

His heart, however, surprised her. It shone with courage and a compelling desire to protect those who were weaker. That part fit what she knew of the origin of red wolves as protectors of the ancient Celtic villages before their corruption by greed, so it wasn't entirely unexpected. The surprising thing was love. He glowed with it. Liliana saw flashes of a golden-haired human man with a gentle smile and a quick wit.

Liliana had not expected a deadly predator to have such a generous heart. The heart she saw did not fit the legends of ruthless mercenaries who killed without conscience. Nor did they match the ugly memories she had of the ones who murdered her parents and many of her family and childhood friends.

"Did you come here to kill me?" she asked him.

He looked away from her face. "Not unless I had to."

That was not completely true. Yes, he had come to question her, to possibly bring her back to talk to Detective Jackson or Sergeant

Giovanni if he could. But he'd come armed to the teeth and expecting a trap. The moment she attacked him, he considered that evidence enough to kill her.

The tall, handsome Fae colonel with the scars knew what Peter Teague was. She saw no evidence in the wolf's mind that he knew his colonel wasn't human, but memories of the officer shielding him from the consequences of hunting Other predators were clear. The colonel covered for him in the past, even when he'd killed with claw and fang. The red wolf felt confident the colonel would cover for whatever Peter Teague had to do to stop a spider-kin from killing his soldiers.

So, the Fae colonel protected him. Let him hunt who he chose. Then all the colonel had to do was ask when he needed someone killed.

Sneaky.

Also brilliant.

The longer Liliana studied the wolf-kin, the more deeply his soul tinged sickly green with fear.

Behind his back where he thought she couldn't see, he twisted his wrists, struggling to reach one of his knives or the Taser in his belt. He conversed to keep her distracted, but each passing moment brought him closer to despair as her webs refused to budge.

Liliana was not an intimidating person. She knew this. She was dangerous, sure, but she was not all that frightening.

You are one of the strongest of beast-kin. Why do you fear me?

She saw the images of the soldier victims in his mind, and her fourth eyes followed them back in time against her will to the moment of their death. Death was hard to see around or past. It always overwhelmed her fourth vision.

"It is a horrible death." Liliana shuddered. "Dissolved slowly from the inside while still alive, screaming silently because damaged vocal cords cannot force out sound." Liliana squeezed closed all her eyes to shut out the horror, but it was too late. She would see the poor soldiers' desiccated faces frozen in silent screams in new nightmares now. The one thing Liliana could never do was unsee.

Peter Teague swallowed hard enough for her to hear.

Focusing on the red wolf, she opened her eyes again, all of them. Sweat beaded on his upper lip. His pulse raced even faster. His breath fogged in small pants in the cold, damp night air. The greenish-yellow tinge of terror overwhelmed his noble soul, giving him a ghostly aura.

To a man who worked on criminal investigations, too much knowledge of a crime was evidence of guilt. Liliana's detailed description of the manner of the victim's death cemented her guilt in his mind. The fact that she immobilized him with her web made the wolf-kin's heart race.

He believed her to be the killer.

And he would be the next victim to die screaming silently.

She touched his cheek. "If I must kill you, it will be quick and clean. Not like that."

The wolf's lips twisted in an ironic grin, but he still glowed with fear. "Thanks, I guess."

She'd failed to reassure him. She didn't know how to communicate that she didn't want to kill someone whose inner face shone with love and courage, even if he was the same kind of beast-kin that killed her family. *He* had not killed them, and she was not going to judge this man by the actions of his kin.

With all her eyes open, the shining soul she saw washed away the memory of ugly death. "You are...beautiful."

"Um...oookay." His mind stumbled in confusion at what seemed to him like a complete non sequitur. He jumped through possible motivations for her comment. She glimpsed images in his mind of serial killers who developed twisted sexual fascination with their victims.

Liliana sighed in frustration. When she planned this trap, the spider-kin believed she would have to kill the red wolf. He knew what Liliana was. If she let him go, she would never be safe again in Fayetteville, or probably anywhere in North Carolina.

But she didn't want to kill him.

Liliana rubbed her arms to ease the chill. Now what would she do?

Killing the brave wolf-kin just because he was inconvenient was not an option. She was ashamed of herself for having thought that way.

There was only one choice. She would have to give up her comfortable home, leave her clients, and begin a new life somewhere else. Perhaps she could tolerate living with a circus again for a time, especially if she could settle in one place, perform in front of holovid cameras instead of staring eyes.

The freedom of flying on the high trapeze and dancing in the sky held only by silken sashes was something she missed. And the cats. Liliana's father and brothers were lion-kin, and her second mother was jaguar-kin, so big cats were like extended family. When her father died, her second mother, Ixchel, carried on the animal tamer act with Liliana's brothers, Jason and Petros. Liliana had often snuck into the cages at night to sleep beside the true lions when nightmares plagued her. The huge, lazy cats always seemed to recognize her as family, cuddling with the strange little spider girl and guarding her sleep as if she were one of their cubs.

Circus life wasn't all bad. Being around big cats again would be like visiting old friends.

She tapped her chin. What should she do with the red wolf? He still believed her to be a killer, so she couldn't let him go until she was far away and safe.

"Are you going to let me go?" the wolf-kin asked, hopefully, as she stood lost in thought.

"I like tigers," Liliana said.

"Huh?"

She had made a mental jump and left him behind. Again. Their last few exchanges could not accurately be called communicating. The more eyes she had open, the more pieces of her mind operated at once and the less her mind worked like a human mind, or like the minds of most Others.

She closed her second and fourth eyes to help focus her mind, isolating herself with him in the tiny island of white light.

"Tigers are beautiful and deadly." She reached up to push a lock of the fierce wolf's bright red hair away from his pretty blue eyes. "I have a tiger in a trap." She ran her fingernails along the side of his scalp as if he were a pet, hoping it would calm his fear. "I do not wish to harm this tiger, but if I let it free, it will eat me."

"I'm not like that." She saw a shading of hurt in him, as if she insulted him by being afraid of him, but the sickly green of his fear faded a bit. Knowing she feared him seemed to make her less scary.

"Celtic wolves killed my parents, most of my brothers and sisters and their children. You are the terror of my childhood." She petted his hair again, because she liked how it felt and because it seemed to calm him.

He ducked his head a little in shame. "I know what Celtic wolves have done, historically, but I'm not them. I'm no mercenary. I'm not even a soldier." His jaw muscles tightened, and he lifted his chin, stubborn pride streaking white-blue through his aura. "I refuse to kill anyone just because someone orders it. That's why I never enlisted, even though both my parents were soldiers. If being different was enough reason to kill someone, then someone should have killed me a long time ago."

Liliana tugged on the silken lines around the wolf's throat to loosen where they cut into his skin. It was hard not to like this wolf. "You believe I'm the widow spider who ate soldiers, so you will kill me."

"You're the only spider-kin I know of in Fayetteville or anywhere around Fort Liberty," he pointed out. He had sensible reasons for his belief. He offered them to her as both explanation and to give her a chance to refute them.

"Spider-kin are rare. I do not believe there are any other seers on this continent." She carefully did not mention her surviving sister and niece in Europe. Better if no red wolf ever knew of their existence. "I only know of one widow spider in North Carolina, but just because I only know of one does not mean there aren't many more. Widow spiders like to nest near each other in groups."

Perhaps Lady Daphne, the widow spider, could explain to the wolf that Liliana could not possibly be the murderer. If he became convinced Liliana was not a killer, he wouldn't hunt her. She also didn't want this orphan wolf to think badly of her.

The wolf's mind considered the possibility he had the wrong spider. "Where can I find this widow spider?"

"Lady Daphne is not your killer either. She lives in Raleigh, which is more than an hour away by car and twenty minutes by bullet train. She only has sex with other women, so she cannot be pregnant." Liliana was not particularly fond of Lady Daphne, but she would not knowingly betray anyone but a bitter enemy to a hunting red wolf. "If you give me your word you will not kill her, I will tell you where she is."

"I give you my word I won't kill her, unless I must to keep her from killing me or someone else," the red wolf swore carefully.

Liliana smiled. Precise oaths like that were the kind sworn by people who kept their word. She told him where in Raleigh to find Lady Daphne's hotel and night club. It was called The Mirror. Raleigh was far enough away from Fayetteville, she doubted Lady Daphne knew anything useful about the soldiers' murders. At least she could confirm the nature of widow spiders, and how they differed from spider seers.

"Is there anything you can tell me that might help me find the real killer?" he asked her.

She could see he still didn't trust her, but he had seen her eyes, all of them. He believed she could see what he could not and was willing to give her a chance to convince him.

She chuckled at the thought she saw form in his head. It wasn't like he was going anywhere in any case.

"Pregnant widow spiders kill only males. You said the widow spider has killed two men?" Liliana asked.

"Six soldiers went missing. Four bodies have turned up so far, and we suspect the others are dead as well, but we haven't found them yet. We could only locate witnesses or evidence for two of the murders, and they both involved a woman who looked like you."

"They were all Others, yes? No Normals?"

"Yeah. That was weird. There's at least a hundred Normal soldiers for every Other. Private Simmons was raccoon-kin. Corporal Araus was crow-kin. The other two we found were Fae of both courts, a seelie sand-djinn and an unseelie pine goblin. So the killings are unlikely to be politically motivated. I don't know about the two soldiers we haven't found yet. I can't test every soldier on the base for divergent biology, but they all reported to Colonel Bennet."

In his mind, Liliana saw the colonel with the scarred face talking to Peter Teague. "Do whatever is necessary. I won't lose any more of my team." The tall Sidhe looked upset and very angry.

"If the widow spider has killed so few men, then more must die," Liliana told Pete, her mind still lingering on the image of the intriguing Fae colonel. "They will all be Others. If she does not consume one Other male each week until she gives birth, her unborn children will begin to die. If she does not feed for too long, then the widow spider herself will die."

She saw his heart that had begun to soften toward her now harden to sharp edges with the wolf's determination to stop her before she could murder another innocent soldier.

Liliana sighed in frustration. The more information she gave him, the more Peter Teague believed she was the murderer he sought.

"Why are you so certain I am the killer?" she asked him. He might refuse to answer, but from five decades of coaching clients in the right questions, she knew it never hurt to ask what she really wanted to know.

He shrugged as best he could with his arms bound awkwardly under her web. "I only have your word for the whole widow spider thing. You're the only spider-kin I've ever met or heard of. You match the general appearance of the killer and know intimate details about the killer's MO. The victims were wrapped in webbing like this, and you're carrying around the murder weapon in your mouth."

"Oh!" Liliana put her hand over her mouth. Her fangs. He believed she was the killer because of her webbing and her fangs. "But my venom is not poisonous!"

"Sure," the wolf said. He didn't believe her.

If she freed this tiger, he would still hunt her down and eat her. She had to convince him she was not the murderer he sought, or no matter where she went, she would spend the next thirty years waking up screaming from nightmares of him coming to get her.

"People seek out spider seers for two things: our sight and our venom."

"You lost me again."

"I am sorry." She pulled on her sleeves, wishing she had chosen a warmer top to wear. "I do not speak in riddles intentionally." Perhaps if she were better at communication, she would be able to convince him with words. Everything she said just seemed to be making things worse.

The only way is to show him.

He was beautiful, both on the surface and beneath. To share venom with him would be a pleasant thing. Once the idea occurred to her, Liliana found she wanted it.

A cold breeze stirred the branches of the pine trees, making her shiver harder. She hugged herself tight and hesitated.

To share venom with someone unwilling was not an honorable act.

To kill him when a less drastic way of convincing him of her innocence existed would be even more dishonorable.

I should choose the lesser evil.

She smiled wide, showing him her fangs. The nightmare was at her mercy. Fear haunted his pretty pale blue eyes. Instead of trying to soothe it, she let herself enjoy the thrill of power it gave her. Her nightmare feared her.

She placed her hand on his chest, over his rapidly beating heart. His throat was tempting to bite, where the pulse raced, but she might puncture a vein that way. Muscle was safer.

"Uh, I thought we were just talking here." The wolf's eyes

widened as she stepped closer.

She felt his powerful muscles bunch and tighten under her hand, but the bonds would hold, even against a Celtic wolf's strength. Liliana had been afraid when she bound him. She'd tied him with enough silk to hold a troll.

"I must show you I am not the killer."

The wolf swallowed, Adam's apple bobbing. "How're you going to do that exactly?"

"I will show you the difference between a bite from a widow spider and the bite of a spider seer."

His voice went up in pitch. "You're going to bite me?" He struggled frantically against her webbing, but it didn't budge.

She smiled with triumph over a hundred years of night terrors. This particular nightmare would never disturb her sleep again.

But this brave man was not a bad dream or a paid killer. She stroked his face. "The venom of a spider seer frees the inhibitions and the mind. It soothes and heals the body. It is a thing normally shared with one who is loved. It will not harm you."

"How about I just take your word for that? You don't have to..."

Liliana shook her head. "That is a lie. You only fear my bite because you still believe it will kill you."

"Well, yeah." He chuckled nervously and licked his lips. "Like you said, horrible way to die."

Liliana pushed the synth-leather of his jacket and some of her webbing to one side and cut the neck of his T-shirt open with her arm blade, baring part of his shoulder. Warm smooth skin soothed her cold hands.

"Can't we, um, talk about this?" Peter Teague squeaked.

Nothing she said would quell his belief that her fangs were deadly murder weapons.

The warm fog of his rapid breaths brushed her cheek as he struggled frantically, even trying to bite her. She stood on tiptoe to reach the thick muscle of his shoulder.

"I do not wish to kill you, nor let you kill me, so..." She bit him.

CHAPTER 7

SPIDER BITE

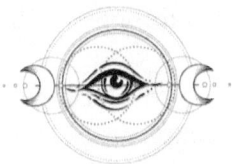

THE WOLF-KIN HISSED THROUGH HIS TEETH AT THE STING of Liliana's fangs piercing his flesh.

She inhaled his scent: faint traces of formaldehyde mixed with damp canine fur and soap. She had not shared venom in many years and never with a man so fierce. The spider-kin strained to the tips of her cold toes to lick the trickle of blood from the two small puncture wounds on his shoulder muscle. The coppery, salty taste made her shudder.

He groaned, and she felt the vibration under her tongue. She looked up at his face with all her eyes, smiling at the confused euphoria there. "See, red wolf. You are not dying."

"If I am, then I'm going to die happy." He chuckled. Then he blinked and shook his head as if trying to clear it. "If you bottled that, you could make a fortune."

"Spider seer venom is worth many thousands of dollars per ounce, but I prefer to make my living in other ways and save my venom for those I choose." Warmth flushed her cold cheeks. "Venom is meant to be shared with a lover, but you already have a lover. I'm sorry it was necessary to bite you, but you wouldn't believe my words." She reached up to stroke the pale eyebrow of the wolf and searched his fuzzy, floating mind and heart. "Do you still believe I am the killer you seek?"

The wolf grinned and touched his forehead to hers where she stood on tiptoe. "I get it. You're a lover, not a fighter."

Liliana stiffened and pulled back at the insult. "I just defeated a Celtic wolf in single combat."

He laughed gently like a teasing friend. "It's just an expression. You're pure class."

Liliana did not keep up well with current slang, but she was fairly certain that was a compliment. The image of her as a killer faded away in his mind. Even under the fog of her venom, Peter Teague understood that her bite could not have killed anyone.

He was still a Celtic wolf though, a hunter of Others. He knew what she was and where to find her. If the Fae colonel who controlled him realized the implications of her abilities, he would want her dead. Simply by existing, spider seers threatened anyone in power who needed to keep secrets. That was why people kept putting bounties on their heads.

Red wolves had killed spider seers far too many times in the past.

In Peter Teague's heart was an overwhelming instinct to protect, especially children, and most especially any man or woman he cared for. It gave her an idea. "Kiss me, and I will free you," she said.

If he kissed her, he would have more of a connection to her. He would be less likely to hunt her. And surprisingly, considering he'd just tried to kill her, she wanted him to kiss her.

The wolf was strong and fierce and beautiful. She only had four years to find a mate before she reached maturity, and the decision was taken away from her by biology. She hadn't thought about her approaching maturity in some time. It snuck up on her.

The wolf hesitated, pale brows pulled together as if he were trying to remember something. It took a strong will to resist the suggestibility of her venom. The red wolf must find her truly repulsive.

Normals found her eyes terrifying, and even most Others found them unnerving. People who saw her with all her eyes open rarely thought of kissing. Screaming and running away was the usual response.

Liliana looked into the wolf to see what held him back, expecting a horrific view of herself. Instead, she saw the wolf's beloved with the gentle smile. Thoughts of him held the wolf back from Liliana. She saw him put a ring in a drawer under his socks. He was just waiting for the right moment to ask his chosen mate to be his for life. He didn't want to kiss someone else and betray his beloved.

His heart was completely given. Even with her venom in his veins, and an attraction to her, he thought only of his boyfriend.

Liliana's own heart warmed at his loyalty to his beloved. It also saddened her, both because she desired him and because her fourth eyes showed that "No" would be the answer when Peter Teague finally got up the nerve to ask. "Your beloved will have a lifetime of kisses from you if he will but say yes. He can spare a single one for me."

The red wolf grinned at her, wide and mischievous. Dazzling. "Okay, one kiss then."

He pressed closed lips against hers, enthusiastic and sweet.

She closed all but the eyes looking into his heart and mind as she sank into the warmth of the brotherly kiss.

In his mind, she saw herself now. He thought she was scary and cute at the same time. Her eyes fascinated him, like exotic jewels embedded in her face. To him, her second eyes looked like polished metallic-jade cabochons in her temples; her third eyes were tiny black pearls. Her fourth eyes looked like opals to him, with their ever-changing swirling surface of pale purple, green, and blue in translucent orbs set above her brows as if in a circlet.

His inner image of her flushed her cheeks warm as much as the sweet kiss. Her eyes did not disturb him. He liked them.

Envy of his golden-haired lover stabbed at Liliana.

With a sigh, she stepped back from him. Any connection she could forge with a single brotherly kiss had been made.

She flexed her wrist to extend her arm blade to cut his bonds.

She had to kill the tiger in her trap or free him, and she didn't want him dead, especially not after she had kissed him and shared venom with him. The line she cast to bind him had caught her in her own trap. Treating this wolf-kin like an enemy was no longer possible. She had to set him free while venom made him docile.

Peter Teague's eyes widened when he saw her blade. Piercing through the fog was an image of her killing him. The venom in his system made it impossible for him to truly feel fear, but his pale brows drew together. "I thought you liked me."

Hurt feelings.

Liliana flexed her wrist to fold her blade back into the nearly invisible sheath in her forearm. The wolf still believed she would kill him, and the kiss was not enough to make her feel safe either. "I do like you, beautiful wolf. I just don't trust you not to kill me in my sleep."

"I wouldn't do that. I'd only kill you when you were awake," he said, with the unfiltered honesty of the venom in his veins.

Liliana chuckled. "I am not reassured, but thank you for trying."

There was nothing for it. Liliana would still have to leave town and disappear. As much as it pained her, she would rather leave her clients unguided than murder this brave wolf-kin. She would have to be somewhere else when he was freed.

Peter Teague did not have one of the wrist phones everyone seemed to have this decade. She felt in his pants pockets.

He grinned and squirmed. "Hey, I thought you knew I was taken."

She found a phone in his jacket pocket along with the spare clips. The phone was possibly older than the wolf. She wondered why he carried such outdated communication technology. Behind his back, where his hands were bound, she pressed his thumb against the screen. Zoe Giovanni was on his contact list. Liliana touched the number and waited. She got voice mail. For a moment, she considered what message to leave.

No. Not safe.

Liliana couldn't leave Peter Teague tied to a tree in the woods for an unknown amount of time, helpless in the cold, until Sergeant Giovanni remembered to check her voice mail.

Celtic wolves had many enemies. Being defenseless at the wrong moment or trusting the wrong person could mean death.

She hung up.

"Besides Sergeant Giovanni," she asked the wolf, "who would you trust with your life?"

"Doctor Nudd," he said without hesitation.

Liliana touched the number for Nudd Home.

"What do you want this time, Pete?" the gravelly voice on the other end of the phone asked. The wolf's phone was not quite as old-fashioned as her push-button corded phone at home, but it was definitely a few decades behind. There didn't appear to be any holographic display, or even a flat video display that she could access, just voices in the dark.

"You are Doctor Nudd?"

"Yeah, who is this? How did you get Pete's phone?" The voice had gone from annoyed to tense.

"He needs your help." Liliana told the voice how to find them. "How soon can you get here?"

"What kind of trouble is Pete in? Is he hurt?"

"He is not seriously hurt." There were two tiny trickles of blood on the wolf's shoulder. Aside from that, he wasn't even visibly bruised from their fight. If he were hurt in some way she couldn't see, her venom would take care of it. "But he cannot defend himself."

"I can be there in fifteen minutes."

Liliana put the wolf's old-fashioned phone back in his jacket pocket with the spare clips for his gun.

She opened her second eyes, closed her third and fourth eyes, and left the tiny island of human visible light to collect his weapons from the forest floor. She remembered to yank the two throwing knives out of the tree and to locate the long knife among the pine needles. The wolf-kin seemed fond of his knives.

"Anna?" he called to her as she walked away into darkness. "You're not going to leave me like this, are you? You said you would let me go if I kissed you."

Liliana placed his throwing knives next to the gun with its tiny bright light. She picked up his sword. It was well-crafted and very old. Liliana held it by the hilt. A fine, balanced weapon. Her hand felt warm on the hilt, and it fit as if it had been made for someone with hands her size. That seemed unlikely since the larger wolf-kin had also seemed comfortable wielding it. In the dark-seeing vision of her second eyes, it glowed softly. It must be enchanted in some way. She had a strong desire to keep the sword, but she had no right to it. Reluctantly, she laid the fine weapon at its owner's feet. "I keep my promises. Your friend, Doctor Nudd, is coming. He will free you."

"Why won't you?"

"I need to go."

"Where are you going?"

"Somewhere far away where you won't find me and kill me."

"You don't have to go. It's obvious you're not the right kind of spider. I'll go to Raleigh tomorrow, talk to Daphne, the widow spider you told me about. If your story checks out, I'll know you didn't have anything to do with the murders, and I'll leave you alone."

"Will you?" Liliana opened her fourth eyes, searching for future intersections between their life paths, but too many random images overlaid each other until she could see nothing regarding this wolf and her. It was like trying to listen to a single conversation while a thousand people talked at once.

Flux.

Her hands curled in frustration. Her fourth eyes always failed her when she most needed their guidance. The very act of trying to make an important decision made a mess of her visions.

Decisions made in the next few minutes would forge the direction of her future, affecting every moment from here forward. There was no way for her to see anything solid until she chose a path, and then it would be too late.

Peter Teague was trustworthy. She had seen into his heart and mind. He was an honorable being who sought to make the world better. He believed he was telling her the truth. But he also seemed completely unaware of the depth of influence the powerful Fae colonel had on his choices.

She certainly did not trust an unknown Sidhe, no matter how nice he was to look at.

She put her cold hands on the wolf's warm cheeks and stood on tiptoe so she could touch her forehead to his again. He bent down to let her. "Farewell, beautiful wolf."

"Pete. My name is Pete."

"Pete." Liliana tilted her head to one side, considering. "My name is Liliana. People mostly call me Madame Anna now because of my sign, but I like Lilly. My father used to call me Lilly when I was little."

Pete smiled, relaxed with the carefree euphoria of her venom's influence. He had such a stunning smile. It made her knees feel wobbly. It had been years...decades?...since anyone smiled at her like that. "Lilly," he said. "I like it."

Liliana caught a dangling silk line and scrambled up into the tree branches, into the darkness his eyes could not pierce.

In minutes, his friend would be there to free him. She should go.

But she didn't.

CHAPTER 8

THE FAIRY AND THE GOBLIN

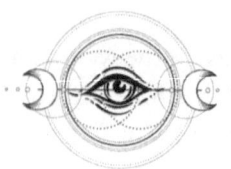

Liliana clenched her teeth to keep them from chattering. She couldn't feel her toes. She needed to get out of there, get somewhere safe and warm and far away before the red wolf got free. Instead, she huddled in a ball on a high tree branch above the little patch of woods where she had trapped him, tucking the hem of her skirt under her toes to protect them from the rough bark.

The ground was now clear so Pete's friend wouldn't trip, but she left many of the higher lines that would allow her to move freely and quickly.

She looked down at the red wolf, bound and helpless in his tiny island of white light.

He didn't look scary.

Liliana studied her feelings, turning them over and over. Was she afraid of him still?

A little. Yes.

Then she should go.

Instead, she watched him from above with all her eyes.

Probably she should watch with her fourth eyes for his friend to come, but she didn't know what he looked like, so finding him with her fourth eyes would be difficult. Besides, she couldn't really focus on anything but the shining figure of the red wolf lit bright amidst the eerie colors of her second sight. He looked...vulnerable. Anyone could kill him if they found him now.

He struggled with his bonds periodically, just out of boredom. He couldn't shift into his larger demi-wolf form with the silken cords tied so tightly, so he couldn't cut or chew his way out. The immediate euphoric effects of her venom should have worn off by now. He was very healthy and young, so he probably wouldn't notice the subtle healing effects until later.

Pete wasn't anything like what she expected of a Celtic wolf.

Conflicting impulses swirled through all the compartments of her mind, leaving her paralyzed.

While she struggled with herself, she heard soft footsteps on the pine forest floor. Two people approached with caution, one near the lower limit of human height, less than four feet tall, the other near the upper limit, over seven feet tall.

Both wore their human forms, but Liliana had all her eyes open. She immediately saw them for what they were: a seelie Fae and an unseelie Fae, a flower sprite and an oak goblin, a creature of sunshine and one of stars. The seelie day court and the unseelie night court were in perpetual cold war that sometimes ran hot, shedding rivers of blood over millennia. She had rarely seen two such opposite creatures in each other's company without one of them dying in the end.

The spider-kin snarled silently and showed her fangs to the dark forest. The little flower sprite, Siobhan, had set the red wolf on Liliana's trail. Now, here she was in the company of an unseelie Fae.

Both the goblin and the sprite crept through the woods with weapons drawn as if expecting a fight. Yet they let their backs show to each other.

The red wolf was the only thing lit in the inky shadows beneath the trees. The two Fae couldn't fail to see him and to see that he was unable to defend himself.

Unseelie Fae were known to go to great extremes in their hatred for Celtic wolves. They would do anything to kill them. They had murdered Pete's parents. If Siobhan were in league with the local unseelie Fae, then this might have been her plan all along.

I got it wrong.

Siobhan's intention had not been to get the wolf to kill Liliana, but to get Liliana to kill the wolf.

She used me.

Liliana had unwittingly given Pete over to his enemies, wrapped like a present.

She measured silk carefully, unsheathed her arm blades, then jumped.

While the seelie sprite would not be able to see in the dark, the goblin would. Like all unseelie Fae, his kind preferred the night. He saw in the same wavelengths as her second eyes. Still, since the sprite carried a compact machine gun, and spider seers were not bulletproof, Liliana aimed for Siobhan first.

A shouted warning from the goblin who saw her coming was expected, but Liliana was almost on top of the small Fae in her human form.

Too late, the little Fae swung the muzzle of her weapon around.

Liliana struck the sprite's hands with the blunt side of her blade, knocking the gun from her grip just as she had done to disarm Pete.

The sprite pulled a handgun from under her black leather jacket while Liliana flipped up, landed on a branch, and jumped for another line. She swung around for another pass from a different direction. The tiny woman pushed on her temple next to her left eye, and the eye began to shine with an eerie green glow.

The dangerous little Fae looked right at Liliana and aimed precisely.

She can see me!

As the barrel of that gun lined up with her chest, Liliana squeaked in terror and let go of her line. She dropped to the ground and rolled, hoping to throw off her opponent's aim.

While running a random pattern between the tree trunks, the spider-kin closed her human eyes, which were useless in the dark anyway, and opened her fourth eyes. She had not yet mastered fighting with them open, but she knew, without the warning of her fourth eyes, she could not be faster than a bullet.

A bullet smacked into the tree beside her. Splinters of wood stung her face. She dodged behind the tree trunk and scrambled up as fast as a squirrel using her spinnerets, her arm blades, and her hands and feet. Her breath came in quick pants, and her heart pounded in her chest. It was too soon for her to be winded. Fear then. Of dying.

Twice in one night.

Her fourth eyes made combat extremely difficult. She might strike where her enemy had been or dodge a weapon that hadn't yet been fired, or wasn't even there.

She fervently wished she had more skill at combat with her fourth eyes open, but it was her only chance.

Perhaps she could manage if both her second and fourth eyes were focused on a single object. She focused as hard as she could on the gun in her small enemy's hand and leapt for a new line.

Pop. The gun went off.

The bullet hit the branch where Liliana had been rather than where she was, but that was her quick, erratic movements saving her. Her fourth vision had not helped. It showed the gun firing in a dozen different directions.

The gun barrel and the small slender arm tracked Liliana again in the now of her second eyes.

An image of the gun firing overlaid the reality.

The spider-kin released her line and dropped, just before another pop and another bullet where she had been.

Yes!

"Damn it, bitch. Hold still," the sprite cursed.

I have absolutely no intention of doing that.

Instead, she grabbed a hanging silk cord with one hand and used it to flip up onto a broad limb. She pulled a loop of silk from her spinneret, then leapt for branches and dangling lines as unpredictably as she could.

As she swung over the little Fae, she dropped the loop over the gun barrel. She saw two images of bullets coming toward her at the same moment and didn't know which one to dodge. One would hit her head, the other her shoulder. She took her best guess and dropped flat onto a tree branch, then rolled to one side just in case she guessed wrong. The bullet hissed past her shoulder, burning her with the heat of its passage.

She'd guessed wrong, but a bullet graze was an acceptable price. She still had her head.

She pulled on the loop.

The gun flew out of the cursing sprite's hand.

Before the petite walking arsenal could pull out another gun, Liliana grabbed a line and swung directly toward her, planning on planting her feet in her small foe's belly.

The Fae sprouted huge dragonfly-like wings through slits in the back of her black bolero-style jacket. Her body shrank as small as an infant human and fluttered upward and to one side.

Liliana's feet missed their mark, but she still felt a thrill of triumph as her abused toes landed in thick, prickly pine needles. She had caused her enemy to make a mistake. Taking to the air was not a wise move in a patch of woods filled with hanging strands of spider-kin silk.

Siobhan's wings flapped into Liliana's dangling lines and tangled. Liliana threw more fresh, sticky silk to further entangle the little Fae in spider-kin web. In seconds, the sprite could barely move her wings, trapped.

Their fight brought Liliana to the edges of Pete's island of light. The Fae had come that close to killing the helpless wolf-kin. Liliana opened her human eyes and looked to make certain he was still safe.

His eyes widened in fear, but he focused on something past her. "Doc, no!" Pete shouted.

With her second eyes, Liliana saw a giant shadow behind her, a massive club lifted to smash her skull.

In one motion, Liliana ducked, twirled to face the goblin, and raised her left arm, sharp blade out. The club struck her blade, not her head. The force of the blow nearly dislocated her shoulder as her blade caught the wooden club and stuck in it. She let the powerful blow spin her around again.

The force of the goblin's strike gave her the momentum to yank the weapon from his sloppy grip. She ended the spin with the goblin's club stuck on her left arm blade and her right arm blade snugged against the goblin's genitals.

"Yield, Fae. I have no quarrel with you, but I will not let you kill this wolf." With her second eyes, Liliana watched the sprite in tiny, demi-plant form. Her delicate wings beat frantically in the web, but she didn't draw another weapon or make any hostile moves toward the helpless red wolf.

"Kill him?" the goblin said, looking confused.

"We didn't come here to kill him, you brainless spider," the flower Fae said in her high-pitched voice. She shifted back to her heavier human form. Her tangled wings vanished, which freed her to drop to the ground.

"Lilly, it's okay," Pete said, chuckling. "That's Doctor Nudd. You called him."

Without moving her arm blade from the goblin's tender parts, she tilted her head so some of her eyes pointed toward the bound wolf. "Your closest friend, the one you trust with your life, is a goblin?"

"Yeah."

Liliana's world turned completely sideways. No version of reality existed where that made sense. "And the fairy?"

"Hey!" the seelie flower sprite in human form called indignantly.

"Yes, Siobhan is my friend too," Pete said.

Liliana stood frozen in confusion, head cocking one way, then the other, arm blade still threatening the goblin's reproductive future.

"Lilly, weren't you going to leave before they got here?" Pete asked gently.

"The world is a dangerous place, especially for Celtic wolves,"

Liliana said, not certain if he would understand why she stayed, or even if she understood why.

She looked at the goblin, opened all her eyes, and studied him. He had the usual core of stubbornness and anger of a goblin, but it was carefully damped and controlled. His soul sang with music and glowed warm with compassion like a hearth fire. He was...kind, if such a word could ever be applied to a goblin.

"You are friend to a Celtic wolf?" she asked him incredulously, watching for falsehood in his answer.

"Yes," the goblin said carefully, her razor-sharp blade still touching him intimately. "I'm his friend. I'm here to help."

Truth.

Liliana backed slowly away from the goblin until her heel touched the toe of Pete's big boot, one blade still held up defensively to the goblin and the sprite. The other blade dragged the huge club stuck to it. She saw truth in the goblin's mind, but she couldn't quite believe it. She had never doubted her eyes before, but this just didn't make sense.

Unseelie Fae and red wolves were the worst of enemies.

In any normal version of reality, the goblin should be trying to kill the red wolf. The best that could be hoped for between them would be an uneasy armed truce. Instead, she saw fond affection, protectiveness, even a fatherly sort of love in the goblin. For Pete.

With a disorienting jolt, she realized where she stood: her back to the red wolf, her blade to the two Fae. She trusted her back more to the Celtic wolf than to the kind goblin or the well-armed sprite. Things had shifted in the twisting maze of her mind so much more than she could process. She needed to go home. She was cold and confused, hungry and tired.

Her blades shook as she shivered.

"Lilly, it's okay," Pete said. "I trust them,"

She looked at the wolf with every eye.

"I'm safe now," he told her.

Liliana looked at the still bound and defenseless wolf and saw truth. Liliana, the spider-kin he had accused of murder and tried to kill, stood there with her blades out. The oak goblin stood there in demi-tree form, eight feet of inhuman strength covered in tough, barky skin and twiggy hair, the scent of past bloodshed lingering in his soul. The sprite stood there too, cute human face creased with irritation, holding her hand where Liliana's first blow had bruised it while taking away her small machine gun.

Pete believed it when he said he was safe. He no longer feared her at all. Nor did he fear the goblin or the sprite. He counted them among his closest friends. What kind of a Celtic werewolf considered Fae of both courts to be his closest friends?

A wolf she did not need to fear?

"Pete," she said, looking into his handsome face with all her eyes. "Am I safe now?"

"Yeah, you're safe too, Lilly. I believe you didn't kill the soldiers." He met her human eyes with his. Her six other open eyes didn't bother him as they often did others. "I'm not going to hurt you."

Truth. She saw pure white truth, uncolored by doubt. It was as real as an oath. He would not hurt her.

His emotions swirled in mixed colors between amusement and embarrassment on the surface for the situation he found himself in, shaded with guilt for trying to kill her when she was clearly innocent and an awed sort of gratitude that she fought to protect him, even after that.

No fear.

She looked down. The intensity was too much to bear for long, like staring into a bright light.

If the wolf didn't fear her, then he wouldn't hunt her unless someone ordered him. And he insisted he would never kill just to obey an order.

She believed him.

A powerful sense of relief swept over her.

It took a hard shake to get the goblin's heavy club off. She flicked her wrists to sheath both blades and stepped aside, letting Doctor Nudd get to Pete.

The goblin started cutting Pete free of her web using one of the sharp knives she left at the wolf's feet.

Liliana stepped back into the shadows, rubbing her arms and shivering. Her arm hurt and sluggishly oozed blood where the bullet grazed her. Her foot hurt where Pete's claw cut the top during their battle.

Now, she could go.

She looked up to find a good hanging line to climb.

"Lilly, wait," Pete said. "Doc, give Lilly your sweater."

"What! I knitted this sweater myself. It took me weeks."

"She's freezing. She's been stuck outside all day with just a thin dress, no coat or shoes. Give her your sweater. She'll give it back. Won't you, Lilly?"

The wolf cast the question into the darkness. He couldn't see her, but he knew she was still there.

"I'll give it back," she said.

The goblin rolled his eyes and grumbled. "You want the sweater off my back now. What's next?" He pulled the thick sweater off over his head and held it out to Liliana. Pete might not be able to see her, but the nocturnal goblin and the sprite with her eerie glowing green eye could see her fine. A soft, mechanical whirring sound came from the eye as Siobhan shifted focus to the spider-kin's new location.

Liliana took the sweater at her arm's extreme reach and hopped back from the goblin warily. She pulled on the garment, still warmed by the goblin's body. The loose red and brown sweater swallowed her petite form, falling clear to her knees. It was heavenly, all soft, thick yarn with no scratchy labels. She pushed the sleeves up to free her hands.

"Thank you," she whispered. That was an easy social rule to remember, to say thank you when someone handed you something, but it meant something more. While the goblin grumbled, she had seen in his heart he was glad to give her warmth, glad he could help someone who had protected his friend so fiercely.

When she glanced at the sprite, she saw a reluctant nod of

respect. "Well fought, spider-kin." Guilt colored the sprite's inner face. Siobhan set the wolf on her trail, and now she regretted it.

Time for Liliana to go. She jumped, caught a line, but she had a strange desire for Pete and his friends to see her leave.

She scrambled up high in a tree and dove onto a line attached to the tree where Pete was tied. She swung around, circling the tree on that long line in a tightening arc until her feet touched the tree trunk itself, just above Pete's head. She leapt then, caught another line, and swung into a high-flying flip as if from a trapeze full in the spotlight of the pistol's LED. Her precise landing on a branch finished it off. She suppressed an urge to bow.

Behind her, she heard laughter and the wolf's voice. "Now, you're just showing off."

Grinning, she ran along the branch as if it were as wide as a road.

Like a squirrel, she leapt from branch to branch, using the lines she left on her way there to swing across the wider gaps. When she dropped down to the sandy path, she opened her fourth eyes. She wanted to see what would happen in that little patch of woods after she left.

The goblin, Doctor Nudd, finished cutting away her webbing to free Pete. The red wolf knelt to collect his weapons.

"She bit you!" Siobhan said, as she noticed the tiny puncture wounds on the wolf's shoulder. "Pete." The little Fae reached up to touch the marks. "Are you okay?" Her sweet voice shook with emotion.

Pete patted the sprite's shoulder. "I feel fine, Siobhan. It doesn't even hurt."

"Lucky you," the goblin grumbled.

"Lucky?" the sprite piped, voice gone even higher with panic. "He's been bitten by a spider-kin. He could die!"

"He's been bitten by a spider seer." The goblin snorted a laugh. "There are people who would pay a fortune for that privilege."

Pete's brows drew together. "Why so much? There are a lot of drugs on the street with a longer lasting high."

"The high is just a side effect," Doctor Nudd said. "Do you have any old injuries that aren't fully healed?"

"My shoulder and ribs still ache from where that troll tossed me around."

"How do they feel now?"

Pete stood, rolled his arm, took a deep breath, and his face lit with wonder. "No pain at all. I feel great."

Doctor Nudd shrank down from a towering oak goblin to his gangly human form. The tall, slender man scratched his impressively bulbous nose and nodded. "Spider seer venom used to be available in Other markets back in the early 1900s and before. It can cure nearly any illness or injury, but it was rare even then and came at a high price. I haven't seen any for sale anywhere in the last, oh, seventy years." His bushy eyebrows drew together, and he scratched his chin. "Hmm. Maybe eighty or more. I thought the spider seers were extinct."

"That is so class!" Siobhan said. "Think I could get the spider to bite me? My left wing aches something fierce when it rains."

"Class?" Pete clenched his jaws, and anger touched his voice. "I could have killed her, Siobhan."

The flower fae wrinkled her pert nose. "Yeah, she's not likely to be in the mood to do me any favors after I sicced a red wolf on her."

"You told me she was the only spider-kin who fit the description and was almost certainly the killer. She's not even the right kind of spider. She said I should talk to a woman called Lady Daphne in Raleigh."

"Daphne?" Siobhan said. "The toff that runs the Mirror Club? She couldn't possibly be the killer. Madame Anna fits the description you gave me. Daphne's not even close."

"But you knew there were other spider-kin in North Carolina?" the wolf pushed.

"Well, right, yeah. Daphne's a spider too, but she's not petite and slender by anyone's measure."

"The only Lady Daphne I ever heard of was Lady Daphne Fairchilde," said Doctor Nudd. "The rather notorious widow spider who was exiled in 1943 after she seduced Vita Sackville-West and three prominent young noblewomen."

"Yeah, that's her," the little sprite said, nodding. "She lives in Raleigh now."

Doctor Nudd hit his broad forehead with a long-fingered hand with lumpy knuckles. "Siobhan, am I to understand you don't know the difference between a spider seer and a widow spider?"

"It's obvious, isn't it?" The three-foot-ten-inch woman in the leather motorcycle jacket and carrot-red mohawk shrugged and holstered her recovered pistol, cleaned of webbing. "Widow spiders don't have all those creepy eyes. But they're both spiders." She shivered dramatically.

The goblin ran his hand through his unruly nut-brown hair, making it stick up in random directions. "That's like saying a lion-kin and a tiger-kin are the same because they're both big cats."

"Well, they'll both rip your throat out if you irritate them," Siobhan pointed out.

Doctor Nudd rolled his eyes. "Next time, Pete, speak to me when you need information about rare beast-kin species."

Pete nodded. "Duly noted. If I need weapons advice, I'll leaf it to Siobhan," he said with a wink.

"Was that a racial slur, Doctor Teague?" the small woman said with narrowed eyes.

"From me?" Pete's face was a picture of innocence.

"Well, you're barking up the wrong tree there, Fido."

"Are you saying I should petal my wares somewhere else?"

Siobhan groaned. "Maybe we should have just left you tied to a tree where you belong, eh, boyo?"

Pete chuckled. "Point taken, Tinkerbell."

The sprite's squeal of indignation rang through the forest.

Liliana let her tired fourth eyes close as the wolf, the goblin, and the sprite continued to bicker and tease each other in the patch of woods she'd left far behind. It was clear Pete believed her now, and neither he nor his Fae friends had any intention of doing her harm.

She went home, to her own home, to her own warm cozy bed, where everything was exactly where it should be.

Instead of nightmares about Celtic wolves coming to rip her to shreds, she dreamed of a smiling wolf with pretty blue eyes who kissed her like a brother and of a gallant goblin who gave her a sweater.

CHAPTER 9

BEDRIDDEN BADGER

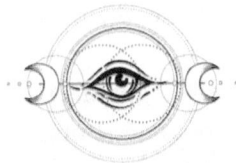

THE NEXT MORNING, AFTER LILIANA CALLED HER CLIENTS from the previous day to apologize and reschedule their appointments, she got to work finishing the cleaning and organizing that had been so abruptly interrupted. She smiled and hummed as she worked, thinking of the handsome red wolf she met, his pretty human soldier friend, the detective who was just her size, and the two mismatched Fae. She also wondered about Colonel Bennet, whose fate was connected to all of them.

He seemed to be the point where all their fates met. Random images of the Fae colonel appeared in her mind in association with each of the new people she'd met. Sergeant Giovanni had the closest association. She'd served with him since the Energy Wars. Her loyalty to him had been unshakable when Liliana looked into the sergeant's soul. Liliana also saw an image of him speaking to Siobhan about making a custom handgun. That's why he'd been at her shop. Several visions showed him with Doctor Nudd seeking advice.

Liliana's own fate was also likely intertwined with his in some way, or he wouldn't keep appearing in her visions. The Fae colonel represented an unknown that could potentially be more deadly than Pete.

But what about Pete? His cordial relationship with the Fae was the most surprising. Especially the part where the colonel protected Pete while encouraging him do a Celtic wolf's traditional job of protecting innocents from predatory Others. But not paying him or coercing him in any way she could see. Sidhe who had red wolves to command usually used money to twist those instincts, to make the wolf-kin into their own pet killers.

On the other hand, working with military police seemed like a job custom-tailored to an uncorrupted Celtic wolf's protective instincts. Pete seemed perfect for it. Red wolves were born and bred to protect, at least in the beginning. Solifu, Liliana's first mother, taught the fall of the red wolves to her daughter as a lesson of caution against the evils of greed. "The love of money is the root of all evil," the Christian bible said, and Solifu imparted that quote as an important wisdom to teach her daughter, using the fall of the Celtic wolves to illustrate.

Liliana did not agree. Some people desired power, lacked compassion, or even delighted in the pain of others. Jealousy, prejudice, selfishness, and even simple spite—evil had many roots. But she didn't know that then. She'd been young and listened raptly to her mother's voice while her spider seer's eyes saw the ugly truth of the example given.

Long ago, when the Green welled up from the earth in potent springs and the whole world pulsed with power and life, the Sidhe ruled the world. Normals with no magic were prey. The Celts made a pact with the wolf-kin in their midst, food and welcome in exchange for protection. To have a red wolf pack in your village meant safety, and the only cost was an occasional sheep or goat. The deadliest Fae were often unseelie, the night Fae. They hated the red wolves who thwarted them from hunting the Normal humans, their "rightful" prey.

Even now, unseelie Fae hated the red wolves and would kill them if given the chance. Seelie Fae took advantage of that by convincing the red wolves that the enemy of their enemies must be their friends.

Red wolves allied themselves with the rulers of the day courts, even though some of them were more dangerous than the unseelie.

In time, the world changed. Technology poisoned the air and water, ripped the earth apart, and the power of the Green faded. Normals came into their own.

Seelie Sidhe, descendants of the ancient land rulers of the day court, sought political power in many lands to bolster the magical power that faded more each decade. For money, the red wolves hunted whoever their seelie Fae patrons ordered them to kill, even Others who did no harm, eventually even the humans they'd protected for generations.

Spider seers knew secrets. And those who rule always have secrets, so Liliana's people were lucrative targets.

Again and again, spider seers, and many Others the seelie disliked, died with red wolf fangs in their throats.

Ixchel, Liliana's second mother, was the only reason one little adolescent spider seer survived the slaughter of so many of her kind. Ixchel smuggled Liliana and her two youngest brothers out of Europe in a lion cage in the 1940s, even as most of her family fought the pets of seelie half-Sidhe Himmler. Liliana's family stood their ground against Himmler's wolves, covering the retreat of their Rom friends, many of whom were fox-kin.

And died.

Red wolf greed nearly made Liliana's race extinct. Only Liliana and her sister, who had fled to Iceland years before while pregnant and unable to fight, survived the slaughter in Europe. Spider seers might still exist in distant parts of the world, but Liliana had not seen any when she looked.

There was no sign of the corruption of greed in Pete's soul though. His soul shone with rich colors of courage, compassion, and love. And he had pretty hair and lovely blue eyes like a clear summer sky. He was really nice to look at both inside and out.

It figures that he is already taken.

She wondered what Pete was doing now, and her fourth eyes helpfully supplied an image. At that moment, he walked into a hospital room. There was a stocky man in a hospital bed. The sound of beeping and a dimness to the light made Liliana wonder what terrible thing happened to the man.

"Hey, Pete! I haven't seen you since you helped us with that infestation of gremlins in Kuwait." The man in the bed gave Pete a broad smile, even though his dusky skin had an ashen, unhealthy look.

"It's good to see you again, John, although not so much under the circumstances. What the heck happened?"

"Wrong place, wrong time. You know how it is." His short-cropped hair was raven wing black, his expression bleak. The words were an obvious avoidance, a clear indication he had no desire to verbally rehash whatever awful thing put him there.

Pete sat down beside him, in a big, boxy, padded chair with a lever, probably designed to fold out for loved ones to sleep beside their injured family members. "I'm sorry, but I can't stay long." Pete's voice held infinite regret.

"No big. Glad you could make it at all. It's good to see you."

"So how you doing?" Pete said, then hit his forehead with his palm. "Sorry. That was a dumb question."

"It's okay. I'm on so many painkillers, I can barely feel it." He held an arm up with tubes running to a machine next to him. "Weird thing is, I'd swear my toe itches but..." The stocky, dark-haired man's voice trailed off, and Liliana looked at the blankets over his legs. The blankets were flat. The lumps over his legs ended abruptly, about knee-level on one side and about mid-thigh on the other.

"John, man, your last e-message said you weren't in a hot spot." Pete ran his hand through his wavy red hair. "You said you barely even went outside the wire."

The injured man's broad face cracked a smile. "I might have exaggerated that a bit. I didn't want you to worry. I was commanding a small unit. We...well, everyone made it back at least. My people even got most of me back." He looked around the room, a vague expression on his face. "It's weird. I passed out on one continent and woke up on another." He shrugged. "At least I didn't get jet lag that way."

"I heard you were in and out for a day or two, so it wasn't as fast as all that."

"But we really are home, right?"

Pete squeezed his friend's hand, the one that wasn't riddled with tubing. "Yeah, we're at Liberty." He gestured out the window at the gray, drippy day. "That's genuine North Carolina drizzle out there."

John chuckled. "Well, that sure hasn't changed." He looked out the narrow window at the water dripping in rivulets on the glass. "This is it then, I guess."

"What do you mean by it?" Pete asked.

"Well, I'm not much of a soldier without legs. Once they get me fixed up..." He took a deep breath like his next words were hard to say. "I'm a civilian." He swallowed. "Never really thought about that. Always wanted to be career military. No clue what the heck to do now."

"You'll figure it out. You're one of the smartest people I know."

John shrugged. "I guess I've got time to think about it."

Pete stood. "I'm so sorry. I've really got to go. Zoe's waiting on me to chase down a lead in Raleigh on a serial killer."

"Stopping a killer? That's a pretty cool job for a biochemist." John grinned at him. Then his face turned thoughtful. "Maybe I could do something like that next." His eyes unfocused, eyelids drooping. "Good seeing you, Pete. Come back when you can."

Pete stopped with one hand on the doorknob. "Is there anything I can get you?"

"Some good barbecue? The real kind with pulled pork and a tangy sauce, none of that sweet tomato-y crap."

"Will do." Pete nodded with a forced smile and left the hospital room.

Sergeant Giovanni waited for him outside. "Your friend okay?"

Pete covered his mouth and gave a laugh that was half sob. "I guess as okay as a guy can be who went from peak physical fitness to double amputee in a day."

Sergeant Giovanni nodded as they walked past a long desk with nurses and monitors. "That's a hard change to adapt to." She stopped at a cooler and got Pete a glass of water.

Pete nodded thanks and gulped down the water. He seemed smaller somehow, like a great weight pulled him down.

She squeezed his shoulder. "I'm all kinds of sorry about Lieutenant Runningwolf, but we have to find our murderer before another body turns up."

Pete nodded and stood up out of the hunch he'd gone into. "Yeah, I know." He took a deep breath. "Thanks for waiting while I talked to him. I just heard they were bringing him here this morning."

"Yeah. I get it. Glad there was someone here that he knew to visit him. Does he have family to call?"

"Like an uncle, I think?" Pete shook his head. "He's always been pretty much on his own, one of the most independent guys I know. He was so proud when he told me he was on command track."

Colonel Bennet came around a corner in the corridor and came face to face with them. "He was," he confirmed. "And he still is."

Pete looked up at the tall colonel curiously. "Really?"

He nodded. "I'll need to talk to Runningwolf first. Ask him about it later." He looked from Sergeant Giovanni to Pete. "Don't you two have a killer to catch?"

"Yes, sir." Sergeant Giovanni said sharply. "C'mon, Pete."

Pete nodded and followed the Sergeant out while the colonel knocked softly on the hospital room door.

Liliana shifted her vision to track the Fae colonel rather than Pete. She wondered what sort of man this handsome colonel was. How would he treat a wounded soldier?

After a soft "Come in," he entered the room, hat in hand.

"Lieutenant Runningwolf."

"Sir." The man in the hospital bed straightened as much as he could against the pillows.

The colonel looked around quickly, standing stiffly at the door.

"The Army put you in that bed, Lieutenant, and we're going to get you out of it. You've got my word on that."

Lieutenant Runningwolf's face scrunched in confusion. "Not sure how that's going to work, sir."

"We've got the best cyberneticist in the country at this base. Doctor Periclum has given me his word that he'll do everything he can to not just get you walking, but running faster than you could before."

A broad smile spread across John Runningwolf's face, then his head tilted and his eyes narrowed. "Full cybernetic limbs are worth more than my pay for the next twenty years. What's the catch, sir?"

"No catch." The Fae colonel sat stiffly on the edge of the chair that Pete had just vacated. "You can still have a medical discharge, but you'll walk out of here on two new legs if that's what you want to do."

"That is so not what I want to do." His grin went crooked. "Well, I do want to do the walking part, but not the discharge part if there's another option."

"I just want you to know there are no strings on this offer. I'd like you to join my unit, but I don't want you to think its a condition of getting new legs. I heard a lot about you and your performance as a field commander from your CO."

John Runningwolf grinned wide. "All lies. Except for the good parts."

"Then they were pretty honest reports," the colonel said with a small quirk of his lips. "I heard you lost your legs because you blew the bridge you were still standing on so your unit wouldn't be overrun."

Runningwolf's face twisted in irritation. "Damn remote jammed."

"Then, while half buried in rubble, you kept firing to keep the enemy pinned until your entire unit was clear. I heard you refused to lie down even when you were pulling out. You were still firing out the back of the vehicle while they were hauling you away with tourniquets on your legs."

The young man in the bed shrugged. "Not much point in my team keeping me from bleeding out if I caught an enemy bullet with my face." He sagged a little, dark circles under his eyes more prominent. "Are you getting at something, sir?"

"Yes, I am. I need a good XO."

"Got it." Runningwolf nodded. "Captain Carter had no intelligence to indicate an ambush there, and she ordered a retreat immediately. She didn't leave us hanging, did everything right. She's solid, sharp, and always looks out for us. She's a good choice."

The colonel huffed a laugh. "She is. We've worked together before and I trust her judgment. But she's already got a command of her own. That's why I want you for the position. She recommends you highly."

"Me, sir?" Runningwolf glanced at the IV stand. "Maybe they spiked the chemical cocktail on me again and I'm hallucinating. I just made full lieutenant six months ago."

The colonel glanced toward the door, making certain they were alone. "And you're a beast-kin. I would like for my second to be Other since a lot of the soldiers in my unit are."

His eyes narrowed. "I have no idea what you're talking about, sir."

"Even if you being tough enough to ignore crushed legs and keep fighting and giving your people smart orders that got them out of a tight spot alive didn't indicate there was some kind of strong, stubborn beast in you, Carter told me."

"What would give Captain Carter the idea that I was some mythical..."

"She's half Fae. Her mom's a djinn."

Runningwolf stopped in mid-sentence with his mouth still open.

The Fae colonel held up a hand. "It isn't going any further. You've got my word on that. In the Special Enemies and Tactics Unit, being a beast-kin just makes you an even better asset to the team."

"Captain Carter's not a Normal?"

The Fae colonel shrugged with a small twitch at the corner of his mouth. "You're not the only one who can maintain the appearance of a Normal, even under extreme circumstances."

"Huh." The man's eyes closed for a moment in a long blink. "Captain Carter's half djinn. No wonder she never noticed the heat."

"Just out of curiosity, are you wolf-kin? Some kind of big cat? Bear?"

"Badger," Runningwolf said. "May not be as big, but way more tough and ornery, pound for pound."

"I'd say you've proven that. Carter put you in for a Medal of Honor."

"Seriously?" His voice sounded half asleep and more disbelieving than excited. He smothered a yawn. "Sorry, sir. They've got me on some pretty strong stuff."

The colonel stood. "Get your rest, Lieutenant. Consider what I said. Doctor Periclum will be by later to assess you for cybernetics. He's kind of an ass, but he's the best, so..."

"I won't take it personally." Runningwolf gave the colonel a half smile as the tall officer nodded and opened the hospital room door. "Sir?"

"Yes?" The colonel paused, pulling the door closed again so their conversation stayed private.

"Are you seriously offering me a position as second in some kind of elite unit?"

"I am."

"I accept."

"Take some time. Make this decision when you aren't on a pharmacy's worth of drugs."

Runningwolf shook his head. "Won't matter. My mom and dad died in the Energy Wars. My mom got the Medal of Honor posthumously. My uncle raised me. He was Delta Force in his younger days. Medical discharge after he took a bullet in the kneecap stopping a terrorist from blowing up a school. Hell, my grandmother was career military. Being a soldier is all I've ever wanted, and you're offering me my military dream job. There aren't enough drugs in the world for me to change my mind on that."

Colonel Bennet huffed a chuckle and nodded. "The job's yours as soon as you're ready." The moment of lightness vanished. "But heal at your own speed first. I've got the right man for the job picked out. I'm not looking anymore."

"Thank you, sir."

"Thank you. There are thirty soldiers alive today because of what you did. We owe you."

"Just doing my job," Runningwolf muttered, as his eyes drifted closed again and didn't reopen this time.

The colonel watched the sleeping soldier for a few seconds. "If I had a hundred like you, I could rule the world." He left, closing the door quietly behind him.

Liliana tilted her head, watching the colonel as he watched Lieutenant Runningwolf. She hoped the Fae colonel did not want to take over the world. That could cause some serious problems for her little town.

CHAPTER 10

NOSY RABBIT

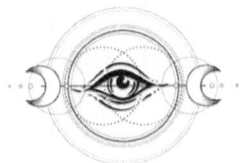

WHEN THE KNOCK ON THE DOOR CAME, LILIANA KNEW IT would be her best customer. Not because she foresaw it, but because it was time for their makeup appointment.

Out of habit, Liliana quickly checked to make sure all but her human eyes were closed and pulled her hair forward before opening the door.

She welcomed Janice Willoughby in with a sweeping gesture and her usual singsong speech.

"Oh, Madame Anna, I'm so glad you could see me," the rabbit-kin blurted before the door was closed.

Janice already knew Liliana was spider-kin, so Liliana opened all her eyes to look at the woman carefully. Janice was an ordinary woman in her late thirties in her human form. She looked exactly like what she was, the harried mother of five active children. In her demi-rabbit form, she was cuter, less careworn, and sleekly furred with large, mobile ears and a twitchy button nose. In her full rabbit form, she looked like an unusually large brown rabbit. "I can see you just fine."

Janice laughed and waved her hands in the air. "Well, of course you can. I just meant I'm glad I could get a makeup appointment so soon."

"What has you concerned?" The spider-kin gestured for Janice to sit with her at the round table with the crystal ball in the center.

"A werewolf came to my house!" Janice shuddered as she sat on the edge of one of the three client chairs and dropped her purse in another. "And not just any werewolf, that would be bad enough, but a red werewolf! Right there on my front porch!"

Liliana looked with her fourth eyes into Janice's recent past and was not surprised to see Pete knock on Janice's door. The spider-kin nodded while Janice rambled on about being terrified and wondering if the beast would eat her children.

The ball in Pete's hands brought him to the Willoughbys' door. One of the new soccer balls with built-in metrics for measuring kick strength, distance, and accuracy. It flashed a light to indicate ideal impact point for various kick angles and sent telemetry data to indicate when it was off sides.

A little more looking around the familiar neighborhood, and a bit further into the past, showed her Pete's golden-haired beloved living next door to the Willoughbys. She watched as one of Janice's children playing in the backyard kicked the soccer ball over the fence into the teacher's yard.

When Pete brought the ball to the Willoughby house, Janice opened the door, smelled the wolf, squeaked in terror, and slammed the door in Pete's face.

Pete's shoulders slumped. He lifted his hand to knock again, then let it drop with a resigned sigh. He left the electronic soccer ball on the porch and went back to his boyfriend.

"The red wolf means you no harm," Liliana told her client.

"How can you be so certain?" Janice chewed on a fingernail and tapped her foot under the table. "Lou saw him at the shop on base too. He's been there to get his van fixed, so he must work at Liberty. And you know how sharp Lou's nose is? Well, Lou swears he smelled blood in an old stain in his van!"

Liliana considered blood stains in Pete's van with her fourth eyes open and saw an image of a much younger Pete gently placing a badly injured Siobhan in his van. "Your husband's nose is correct. The blood belongs to a fuchsia sprite."

Janice covered her mouth in horror. "What kind of monster would kill a harmless little fairy?"

"Harmless" was not a word Liliana would use to describe Siobhan. She snorted. The diminutive warrior had very nearly killed her the day before. "The sprite is his friend. The red wolf was taking care of her after an injury." Her curiosity was piqued, but she would search for more details on Siobhan's injury another time. For now, she owed Janice her attention.

"Is he a danger to my children?"

For the sake of her best client, she looked and broadened her focus question beyond the red wolf who she already knew would never hurt a child.

Is there any danger to Janice's children?

She saw some deadly Other predators prowl their neighborhood streets, but the scent of Celtic wolf-kin, the guardians of humanity and servants of the seelie daylight Fae, made most leave as stealthily as they came. A few predators braved the wolf's scent and met the red wolf himself. That tended to be a violent, occasionally fatal encounter for the predator. "The Celtic wolf loves the Normal man who lives next door to you and teaches at your children's school on base. The red wolf guards his beloved's territory from other predators..."

A rare few deadly Others through the past few years deliberately hunted Pete and also met ugly ends, as they should. But while Celtic wolves were strong, there were many stronger Others.

Do any pose a danger to Pete?

Janice hadn't asked that question, but Liliana worried about the brave red wolf, now that she had begun to know him and saw the dangerous life he led.

It was difficult to pinpoint the moment in time without reference, but the vision was vivid. It had the feel of something in the very near future, within a week or less.

On some overcast night soon, an ordinary-looking man would

creep across the Willoughbys' lawn toward their neighbor's house, avoiding the light from the windows. He wore jeans and a dark blue jacket and had curly black hair worn long, as was the modern style. Only the black band with an embossed silver crown on his muscular neck marked him as unusual.

The Order of the Wolfhound!

Most of the Wolfhounds were wolf-kin, dog-kin, or some other canine beast-kin, and they were all particularly trained and magically enhanced to kill Celtic wolves. They'd also kill anyone else who dared to stand between the unseelie and their "rightful" prey. Wolfhounds served only one royal Sidhe family. Liliana only knew of two living members of that family. One was Titania, the Queen of Air and Darkness, the most powerful unseelie Fae in the Western world, land bonded to most of Europe. The other was her daughter, Aurore Principessa, who had lived more than three centuries but had not yet been chosen by any land.

The curly-haired assassin hunted the quiet suburban streets of Janice Willoughby's neighborhood, undoubtedly on the trail of Liliana's favorite red wolf.

The vision was of the future, but not that far. Liliana held her breath in fear for her new friend. Pete did not have the needed magic to defeat such an enemy. If the Wolfhound found his prey, Pete would die.

Liliana did not have any way to pierce a Wolfhound's protective magic either. If this assassin sought to kill Pete, Liliana would be helpless to stop him.

Instead of Pete, the Wolfhound met a tall, broad-shouldered man with a familiar, burn-scarred face, wearing a maroon button-down shirt and crisply creased black slacks. Liliana recognized the handsome Fae colonel, even though he wore no uniform. His sharply erect stance and buzzed short haircut still marked him like a neon sign as military. Colonel Bennet stood in the light of a streetlamp on the sidewalk in front of the Willoughbys' house, tall and regal in the proud way he held himself.

A quick glance at the colonel's wrist phone showed the date, only four nights in the future. And the time, near midnight, the peak of unseelie power.

She tilted her head, studying him in the brilliant light and deep shadows. A man of contrasts, as beautiful as a mountain, his face nearly as cold and remote.

He called to the Wolfhound with a voice resonating with the power of the deep earth, beyond his normal smooth baritone, a bass rumble of a command with magic to back it up. *"Obaudio me, servus."*

Liliana recognized the Latin. Her father taught her both his native languages, Latin and Greek. "Attend me, servant," the words meant.

Was the wolfhound working for the Colonel?

From what she'd seen, she thought the colonel knew of Pete's nature and accepted him, even protected him. She had assumed he must be a seelie Fae, traditional allies of the Celtic wolves. But the colonel called the Wolfhound, and the wolf-kin, from the order of assassins created specifically to hunt red wolves, came.

The wolf-kin circled the colonel growling, as if uncertain if he should attack or run. "Who are you to dare call me off the hunt in the old way?" The werewolf shifted from human to demi-wolf form. His fangs and claws grew long. Black and charcoal gray fur spread across his skin. His posture hunched into a two-legged crouch.

The colonel stepped out of the circle of white light from the streetlamp into the thick shadows under a big old oak tree in the Willoughbys' yard. His dark clothes and dark skin would make him virtually invisible if one of the Willoughby children happened to look out their window in the dead of night. The shadows seemed to thicken and embrace him, concealing him even more effectively from prying eyes.

In the shadow, the colonel transformed. He added over a foot to his already impressive height, and his handsome face changed to an inhumanly beautiful image carved out of translucent obsidian, flawed only where the scars had marred his human skin. A row of sharp, silver, backswept horns accented his brow like a deadly crown. He flexed forearm muscles carved from black stone, and silver claws extended from his fingertips. Silver needle teeth glimmered in the unseelie Fae's mouth when he gave the Wolfhound a cold smile.

Liliana gasped. Surely that was some sort of glamour. Of all the many varieties of Fae, only Titania and her daughter, Aurore, had silver horns in the shape of a crown. It was the trademark of that royal Sidhe family. But the unseelie queen had no family in this land. That was one reason why Liliana, and so many European Others, fled to the New World. There were no Sidhe here of either the court of night or day to fight over the land's favor.

The assassin's eyes widened. "Your Highness!" The Wolfhound was a peak predator made of sleek muscle, trained in the deadliest arts and protected from most harm by dark magic. He dropped to his knees before what appeared to be the one thing he feared and obeyed, an unseelie prince of Titania's lineage.

"Forgive me," he growled, voice only partially human and accented with something from the part of Europe bordering on Russia. "I did not know any member of the royal family lived in the United States."

Looking like an elegant piece of the night sky come to life, the shimmering black Fae accepted the wolf-kin's obeisance as if it were his right to have Others kneeling at his feet. "I forbid this hunt. The red wolf is not to be touched."

"But Princess Aurore ordered me to..."

A hand made of unforgiving stone with razor-sharp edges struck the wolf-kin across the face. The blow knocked the Wolfhound back onto the concrete sidewalk. "My sister does not rule here," the obsidian Fae said softly, with no trace of emotion in his voice. "I do."

The assassin sat up. His long, pink tongue caught a trickle of blood from the corner of his toothy mouth. The blood was the final proof. The leather collar embossed with the silver crown, provided by the queen's own hand, protected Wolfhounds from most forms of physical harm. Only one of the same royal blood could so easily pierce that protection.

No glamour concealed the Fae's true nature. Colonel Bennet was exactly who he appeared to be: an unseelie Sidhe prince, a son of the Queen of Air and Darkness.

Liliana shivered and twisted her skirt in her hands.

Janice Willoughby bit her thumbnail but didn't interrupt Liliana's vision.

A Sidhe prince lived in Fayetteville. A Sidhe prince with the potential to bond with the land and bring the bloody Fae wars to this continent lived on the Army base, only a few blocks away from her. Liliana considered again her impulse to pack up and move to the other side of the country.

But she fought a Celtic wolf in single combat just the day before for the right to stay in her home. She lifted her chin in defiance, even though the Fae prince could not see. She was not Fae. She owed Fae royalty neither allegiance nor enmity. And the unseelie Fae had, historically, been less hostile to Liliana's kind than the seelie courts. The Queen of Air and Darkness had never sent her Wolfhounds to hunt spider seers.

Plus, she did not know this man. Just as Pete differed from the packs who slaughtered Liliana's family, so this unseelie Fae prince was likely to be different from the seelie rulers who ordered the slaughter of her kind.

She would watch him, but if this obsidian prince offered her no hostility, she would do the same. And if the colonel *did* intend her harm, well then, she would consider whether it would be wiser to flee or to kill him. Sidhe without a bond to the land were not so very formidable. She could probably defeat one if she chose her ground carefully.

She would not give up her home lightly.

The visions of the future fractured at that point, divided into different future possibilities. It was a turning point, a moment when one small decision could fundamentally change all future paths from there.

One branch resulted in serious injury or death to the Fae colonel. The Wolfhound, enraged by the strike, would attack the Fae prince, surprising and killing him. But battles were rarely that simple. So many confounding factors meant the Fae might have a chance to fight back. In those visions, a brutal battle drew blood on both sides, but usually Colonel Bennet won. Even then, he paid for his victory with severe injuries.

This possibility flickered in and out of future existence like the light of a candle in a breeze, one moment most likely, the next impossible and vanished from her future sight, replaced by another equally likely but utterly opposing future.

This usually meant that something between now and then would shift the balance of probabilities so that one future would become the most likely and the other would cease to be possible.

In the other alternate future vision, the Wolfhound would not attack but would instead be subservient to this unknown scion of the family he served.

Liliana watched that branch of future possibility.

"Please forgive me, your Highness," the wolf-kin whimpered, his eyes on the prince's feet. He arched his neck to one side to expose his throat in submission. On hands and knees, he crawled backward out of the tree's shadow, putting himself out of arm's reach of the deadly Fae. "But I serve the princess. She is not known to show mercy for failure."

Mercy was not a word Liliana had ever heard associated with Titania's daughter. Princess Aurore's punishments made the Goblin King's predilection to roast his enemies alive and eat them seem...unimaginative.

Magnanimously, the prince inclined his head to the assassin. "I will speak to my sister. I will let her know this red wolf is under my protection."

The Wolfhound gasped in shocked surprise.

Liliana gasped with him.

An unseelie prince protected a Celtic wolf? That fit with what Liliana had seen of the colonel and Pete's relationship. But the

Order of the Wolfhounds had been created by the unseelie queen specifically to combat the threat of the red wolves.

Pete violated all her expectations of Celtic wolves. His best friend and mentor was an unseelie goblin, and apparently, an unseelie prince protected him.

Janice gasped too, hand over her mouth. She could not know what Liliana saw, but the spider seer's reactions made her foot tap the floor rapidly.

Like a person might do when trying to make friends with an unfamiliar dog, the dark prince extended a hand to the Wolfhound, fingers down, the back of his hand facing the assassin.

Hesitantly, the wolf-kin crept back into the deep, strangely moving shadows of the oak tree in Janice Willoughby's yard, his belly all but scraping the ground, drawn to the commanding black silhouette of the Fae prince. "Thank you, your Highness."

The prince stroked the assassin's hair, dark curls winding around long, slender, clawed fingers, resembling living volcanic stone. "You have only done as you were ordered. There is no fault." His hand tightened in the wolf-kin's hair. He pulled the assassin's head back painfully until the wolf-kin looked up at him.

Softly, the wolf-kin whimpered, but he made no move to defend himself. His eyes slid away from the prince's. He licked his lips.

The tall prince bent down. His black eyes shimmered red in the deep shadows as if lit from within by fire.

Obeying the unspoken order, the werewolf met those fiery eyes for a moment, his entire body quivering in terror.

A silken deep voice purred softly. "I'm curious. My sister would not send an assassin all the way to the United States to kill a red wolf simply for existing."

"I...I cannot speak for my lady. I do not know her reasons."

Twisting the hair in his hand, the Fae prince arched the wolf's throat back until he whined. "You must have some theory of your own," the deep voice purred conversationally. The fiery eyes spoke of barely contained rage, but Colonel Bennet's voice gave away nothing.

"A sword! Princess Aurore told me to search the red wolf's house, slay the wolf and anyone else there, and bring any sword I found to her."

"A sword." The obsidian prince's eyes narrowed. "Why is a sword so important?"

"She didn't say, your Highness. I swear I don't know why she wants it."

"I believe you."

The wolf-kin sagged with relief.

With his free hand, the prince lashed out, crushing the wolf-kin's windpipe with a single lightning-swift movement.

He tossed the choking, dying wolf-kin to the ground and gestured with his hand. The roots of the oak tree moved like the tentacles of a giant octopus, wrapping around the wolf-kin's limbs, even as he struggled frantically.

The prince closed his hand and moved it downward.

The earth moved, making way as thick roots pulled the werewolf underground. He opened his mouth, trying to scream despite his crushed larynx, and a big root shoved between the canine fangs. It emerged out the back of the werewolf's neck in a fountain that turned the churning soil to mud. It was black in the shadows, but Liliana's imagination knew it should be red. Dirt covered the wide-eyed face as the roots pulled the assassin deeper. One clawed hand scrabbled frantically at the oak tree's trunk, leaving deep gouges in the bark, then it, too, was pulled beneath the earth.

The obsidian prince flattened his hand and waved it in a smoothing motion.

After a moment, the oak tree stilled, and the grass crept back across the disturbed ground. The suburban lawn was left greener, but otherwise the only sign the deadly Wolfhound had ever been there were a few scratches in the tree trunk.

In this possible future, the unseelie prince staggered and leaned against the tree for a moment. He shook his silver-crowned head as if to clear it.

Liliana tilted her head sideways in assessment and watched the unseelie prince for a moment more as he recovered from the costly earth magic.

What an interesting person.

Twice in visions, she had seen him kill, once to protect Sergeant Giovanni and now to protect Liliana's favorite red wolf. She felt an odd thrill in her belly at the thought of her life path crossing more with his. Sidhe royalty of any court were always dangerous, but the unfamiliar sensation she experienced felt far more warm and tingly than fear.

She couldn't help but see again the way his eyes once followed a drop of water into her modest cleavage, or that moment when he told her he wished he could believe her, a drop of rain dripping from his hat.

On the future night four days from now, Janice's children would sleep undisturbed if the second vision she saw came to pass.

Next door, in the arms of his human beloved, Pete lay safely, unaware of the death he had narrowly avoided.

As she watched, warmed by the sweet scene of the two men cuddled together, a momentary flash of bloody horror interrupted the vision. Blood splattered the walls. Pete's beloved lay on the bed staring at nothing from dead eyes, his chest ripped open, rib cage hollow, the blankets soaked in scarlet.

Pete fought like a madman, throwing the assassin through walls and hitting him with his furniture, but nothing he did could so much as muss the assassin's fur beneath its magical protection. The Wolfhound laughed as he ripped into Pete's throat with his claws.

Liliana blinked her fourth eyes, shuddering in horror, and the vision shifted back to the other possibility. Pete slept peacefully, his arms warmly embracing the man he loved.

Out in the Willoughbys' yard next door, the crown of silver horns shrank into the colonel's skull as the unseelie prince shifted back to his human form. The shimmering, translucent obsidian skin faded to deep, polished mahogany brown. Colonel Bennet nodded tightly, as if satisfied, and took a steadying breath. Slowly, with great effort, he straightened to his original knife-blade straight posture.

Only a slight trembling in his hands betrayed the exhaustion his use of powerful magic caused.

The colonel was the key. If he survived his encounter with the Wolfhound assassin, Pete and his beloved would be fine. They would never even know they'd been in danger.

"Well, is he?" Janice asked the spider-kin when she could stand the suspense no longer.

Liliana blinked. "Is he what?"

"Is the Celtic wolf a danger to my children?" Janice asked again, fond exasperation in her tone.

"I see no danger to your children in the near future." Liliana gave her best customer a sheepish smile. "I am sorry. I got a little lost in other times and possibilities."

Janice sighed and sat back in the chair across from Liliana at the round table. "That's a relief. I still don't like having a red wolf spending so much time right next door though. And with Lou too." Almost as an afterthought, she asked, "The werewolf won't hurt my Lou, will he?"

Pete would not harm the shy rabbit-kin mechanic, but out of duty, Liliana looked for intersections between Lou Willoughby's life path and Peter Teague's.

A pack of wolf-kin, coyote-kin, and hyena-kin all in full canine form chased the rabbit-kin mechanic in his human form. The pack all wore black collars with embossed silver crowns. They were all members of the Order of the Wolfhound.

Pete ran on Lou's heels in demi-wolf form. The red wolf was not one of the hunters, but a shield to the innocent rabbit, guarding his retreat with bared fangs, claws, a pistol, and knife after knife bouncing harmlessly off his enemies' thick fur. He got the rabbit-kin to safety, then turned to face the wolf pack alone.

Pete fought valiantly, but his weapons and claws could not pierce the pack's protective magic, nor could even his specially made bullets. The highly-trained assassins were skilled fighters and fought cooperatively. The red wolf didn't stand a chance. While Liliana watched, Pete was torn to pieces.

Liliana slammed her fourth eyes shut and gagged, stomach heaving. She swallowed hard.

That vision had the overbright, washed-out colors of a future vision, several months ahead in time at least. The image flickered and faded in and out, as if it were not a likely future.

Reassured by that thought, she risked another look.

What are the alternative possibilities for that moment?

For Janice Willoughby, the other, more likely future was even worse. The Wolfhounds ripped her husband to bloody shreds with no one to protect him.

Liliana covered her mouth in horror.

If he defended the rabbit-kin, the beautiful red wolf would die, but Janice's husband would die if he did not.

"What is it? Tell me what you see, Madame Anna," Janice demanded.

Liliana closed all her eyes tight.

The future she'd seen was not close or certain. There was still time to help steer the rabbit-kin and the Celtic wolf onto a path that would allow both Pete and Lou Willoughby to survive.

Liliana consoled herself with that thought, chanting in her head, *This fate is not set. The future is never certain until it becomes the past.* It was something her first mother and her older sister both said often, whenever they saw a dark future possibility. She gulped in deep breaths to calm her jangled nerves.

Inside her mind, the screams of the good-natured rabbit-kin mechanic still rang. His blood and Pete's stained her inner vision.

"The red wolf is the opposite of a danger to you and your kin." Liliana twisted the fabric of her skirt between her fingers. "Trust him. Danger will come to your husband some time before a year has passed. If the red wolf is there, he will protect your Lou. He will sacrifice his own life, if necessary, to keep Lou safe. If he is not there, your husband will die."

"Oh." Janice's eyes got very big. "I shut the door in his face."

"You must make amends for that social offense," Liliana advised her. She wondered what path would help to make certain Pete would be there when Janice's husband needed him. The image of the Celtic wolf protecting the rabbit had been very flickery, very unlikely. "Be kind to your Normal neighbor, the golden-haired man who teaches your son."

"I'll bake a cake for the PTA!" Janice exclaimed.

Liliana's lips twitched with amusement, piercing the dark mood of the bloody visions lingering in her mind. Every person used the talents they were given. If her husband's life could be saved with excellent cooking, then Janice Willoughby was uniquely qualified.

"Your cakes would make even the fiercest Other into an ally." Liliana patted her hand, a brief, rare gesture.

Janice blushed at the compliment. "Will it really work? Will that be enough to make sure the Celtic wolf protects my Lou?"

Reluctantly, Liliana opened her fourth eyes again.

With Janice following a path to friendship with Pete's beloved, will Pete be there to protect Lou?

The image of the lone red wolf standing against the vicious pack of killers while the rabbit-kin escaped still flickered, barely possible.

Liliana cocked her head to one side, wondering. That should have worked. Janice would follow her advice. Liliana had guided Janice for years.

Why is the future where the red wolf protects the rabbit-kin still so uncertain?

An ugly image assaulted Liliana. Powerful, brutal, and vivid. Close in time and almost certain.

Liliana jumped up onto her chair. She lifted her hands to defend herself. Her reflex was to extend her arm blades, but the danger wasn't to her. She squeezed her fourth eyes shut, but she couldn't shut out the image of Pete's lovely blue eyes, wide and staring with death, his face twisted in a silent scream of agony and horror, his body wrapped in a spider-kin's web. It was the one death that genuinely terrified the brave wolf: death by widow spider bite.

It would claim him soon, probably today.

"No," Liliana whispered.

"What is it?" Janice asked, fear in her voice. "Is my Lou going to die?"

"No, no, no!" Liliana said more forcefully. She jumped off the chair and retreated to the corner of the room by the inner door. The spider-kin turned her back on her best client and twisted the fabric of her skirt until it nearly tore. "No more questions today. I am tired."

It was what Liliana said to clients who stayed too long. Janice had not been there that long, but Liliana desperately wanted her to leave.

"But...um...okay."

With her face in the corner and her back to her client, Liliana watched Janice pull a pay card out of her purse. Liliana hadn't noticed until that moment that she'd opened her second eyes, the ones she used in combat to see all around. They sometimes opened instinctively when she was frightened or upset.

Janice punched a number into her wrist phone, authorized it with her thumb print, and dropped the pay card in the elaborate jar Liliana kept beside the round table. People used to put paper folding money in the jar. Now they put pay cards in it. Barely anyone used paper money anymore.

"I have to know though, Madame Anna." The rabbit-kin hesitated at the door. "Is my Lou safe? Will the Celtic wolf protect him?"

"If the red wolf dies..." Liliana swallowed the lump in her throat and leaned her forehead on the corner walls. "If he dies, take your husband and your children and move away to another city. Without the Celtic wolf, Fayetteville will no longer be safe for your family."

"What's going to happen to him? The red wolf, I mean."

With a bitterness the rabbit didn't deserve, Liliana wondered why Janice cared what happened to the wolf-kin she had so callously rejected. "No more questions today. I am tired," she repeated.

"Can you see me again next week?" Janice asked.

Visions of Pete's gruesome death consumed every part of Liliana's mind. Her hands shook as she ran the fabric of her skirt through her fingers again and again. She barely heard the question Janice asked. It didn't matter. All that mattered was that Pete would die.

Horribly.

Today.

Face to the corner, the spider seer crouched down, trying to block out the sight of Pete's staring eyes. Pete's screaming mouth. Pete's sunken pale cheeks. She squeezed down in the corner into as tiny a ball as she could and rocked, hands over her first, third, and fourth eyes.

Janice Willoughby left at some point.

The day her parents died, Liliana saw it, even before it happened. She watched her eldest brothers and their children, her father, and her first mother all torn apart. She had seen it like a record stuck in a bloody groove, a slice of time looping again and again uncontrollably through her mind. Blood and death and screams, over and over. The family she loved reduced to meat and blood. At that age, she had not yet divided her mind into compartments to separate each vision and shut out what she didn't want to see. She couldn't stop the visions. She was paralyzed by the overwhelming horror. Helpless, useless, trapped in her own mind. Only shutting her mind down completely, going into the blank place where there was no time, could make it stop.

Liliana had only just begun to know the compassionate red wolf. Already she had seen him die twice and seen an assassin murder his strongest protector, the handsome Fae colonel. She felt a surge of unreasoning anger toward Janice. Why had the stupid rabbit woman made her look?

She opened her fourth eyes a tiny slit to look at Janice's future, half-hoping she would see something awful happen to her. Instead, she saw the rabbit-kin baking batch after batch of cookies, along with the cake she had already promised. With a look of stunned delight, the golden-haired teacher who owned the red wolf's heart accepted the generous gifts for his bake sale fundraiser.

Janice's attitude toward the red wolf and his beloved had

radically changed. Liliana saw a potential future flicker into uncertain possibility where a deep friendship developed between the rabbit-kin homemaker and the Normal teacher. That possibility hadn't existed until Liliana spoke to Janice. The rabbit-kin's path altered, as had her husband Lou's by extension and their children's. Liliana now knew the fate of the Willoughby family was intertwined with the fate of the Celtic wolf and his boyfriend. With her advice to Janice, Liliana changed Pete's future in a small way for the better.

It reminded Liliana that she wasn't helpless this time, like she'd been when her family was slaughtered. She could change what she saw.

She risked a quick glimpse into the future, but saw the same three ugly deaths, one close in time and nearly certain, one in a few days if the Fae colonel died trying to protect him, and the other waiting to claim the red wolf in less than a year if he somehow escaped the first two.

She had helped a little, but Pete was still going to die.

Liliana stopped rocking and stood up.

Not if she had anything to say about it.

CHAPTER 11

TOWERING ENEMY

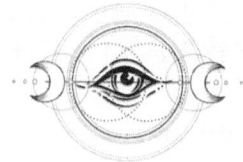

To get from Fayetteville to Raleigh, Liliana had to take an auto-cab. It would cost far more than a simple one-hour ride in a car should, especially now when clean fuel was virtually free and cab drivers were computers that didn't need salaries, but it was necessary. Liliana could not cram herself into the hollow tube of the bullet train to Raleigh with hundreds of strangers and hope to emerge on the other side still sane, and she had never learned to drive or bought a car—so, a cab.

She wrapped a bright red scarf decorated with sequins around her head where it would cover her fourth eyes. She could open and close them freely that way, and since they saw things that weren't in front of her, the scarf would not interfere with her vision. She braided her hair with it in the back so it would be out of her way if she had to fight. Then she walked down the busy street in front of her business, looking for a cab going to Raleigh. She didn't care who it intended to take to Raleigh. Her mission to save Pete was of paramount importance, and time was limited.

She searched for some time as she walked to the nearest busy intersection, then kept walking further toward the center of town. It took nearly half an hour to find a cab. It had just come from the airport in Raleigh, and therefore, it would accept a multicity fare to take her back.

The only problem was that it would be fifteen minutes before it finished dropping off its passenger. Unwilling to wait, Liliana stepped in front of the cab. Its tires squealed only a little. Computer vision, collision sensors, and other recent advances made standing in front of a moving car frequently safter than riding in one.

When the car stopped, Liliana stayed in front of it, following when it tried to back up or go around her.

Finally, the passenger door opened. An angry man in blue jeans with long, black, curly hair got out, shouting at her in what sounded like...Polish, maybe? Slovakian? It had been a long time since Liliana lived in Europe. She not only didn't understand the words, she wasn't sure of the language. However, the man's intention and emotion were very clear as he shouted at Liliana and waved his hands at her to get out of the way.

Once the passenger door was open, the car would not move, so she went around to where the man stood, red in the face from his anger.

With a start, she recognized the man. A bit of black leather collar showed above his shirt despite the long hair mostly covering it. He was the Wolfhound assassin she'd seen in her vision.

She considered killing him right then to prevent the ugly future she'd seen, but they were in the middle of a street in broad daylight. She might have risked it anyway, but a quick peek with her fourth eyes showed her that if he didn't report his arrival at the hotel, another assassin would be immediately sent.

She couldn't remove the threat now, but it helped her to know he was a horrible person who killed without mercy on command. She didn't like inconveniencing anyone by taking their cab, but in the case of this man, she felt zero guilt. He could walk the remaining eight miles to his hotel.

She walked up to him but stepped a few feet away from the car, like she intended to talk to him, and waved him over.

He let go of the car door and stepped toward her to growl and snap unknown obscenities directly into her face.

She sidestepped the man, jumped into the car, closed and locked the door. "Go to the Mirror Club in Raleigh," she instructed the car.

"Override previous destination?" the polite feminine voice of the car asked.

"Yes, please."

The man with the curly black hair pursued her and pounded on the cab roof in fury for a few seconds before the car merged with faster traffic, leaving him behind.

Liliana noticed a large backpack in the seat next to her and assumed it was his. She pressed the button to roll down the window and tossed the backpack out the window.

She found it weirdly satisfying to see it hit the street at speed, roll through a big puddle, and smash into a curb, bursting at the seams with clothing and personal items scattering.

On the other hand, she suspected that her actions would have consequences. As the car pulled into the all auto-drive lane on the highway and accelerated to far higher speeds, she checked the vision she'd seen where the Wolfhound faced Colonel Bennet. As she suspected, the future where the assassin showed subservience rather than rage was gone.

Liliana's recent actions pushed the assassin's anger level beyond control. She sighed. It had been satisfying, but now, even if she managed to save Pete today, he would die a few nights later.

And even if she helped then, he would die within a year protecting Lou Willoughby.

Keeping Peter Teague alive was practically her new hobby.

She sighed again as the beauty of the heavily forested, kudzu-overgrown North Carolina countryside sped past her window. Much of the damage done to the earth by modern technology had been mitigated by the invention of even better, more earth-friendly technology and a shift in attitude that valued the green world rather than disregarded it. But no one had figured out how to get the invasive kudzu under control. It was the sort of problem that a land-bonded Sidhe could fix, but there weren't any in North America.

Pete faced death today because he was following her advice to talk to Lady Daphne Fairchilde. A few days from now, his death and the death of the Fae prince who protected him at the hands of the Wolfhound had both become certainty rather than possibility because of her cavalier treatment enraging the assassin.

These two possible deaths were both her fault. And while she didn't know how the incident that involved Lou Willoughby might be her fault, she wouldn't be terribly surprised if it turned out to be so.

Saving Pete would not be nearly as frequently needed if Liliana didn't keep unintentionally making his already dangerous life even more dangerous. A Celtic wolf who hunted killers did not need her to make his life harder.

The drive took nearly an hour. She looked for various ways to help but hadn't yet found one with the outcome she hoped for.

When the cab dropped her off in front of the Mirror Club, it did not request payment. It took Liliana a moment to realize that because she changed the destination while the assassin was still the logged passenger, the machine automatically charged him for the trip.

She chuckled to herself as she stepped out on the sidewalk, but her laughter died as a pedestrian jostled her. This part of Raleigh was far too busy.

Her heart pounded as more and more strangers walked past, too close.

She looked around frantically, then stepped into a sheltered alcove beside the nearest building to catch her breath. The Mirror Club, owned by a woman she hadn't seen in nearly a century, occupied the building across the street that rose up to an impressive twelve stories.

Lady Daphne Fairchilde, the widow spider, was neither particularly fair nor a child, nor by many definitions was she a lady.

Liliana always found it odd when names didn't match the people who were named.

Now, she faced Lady Daphne's tall building, noting that only the first two floors were the Mirror Club, one of the most popular nightclubs in Raleigh. The upper floors of the building seemed to be a different business, a hotel with balconies overlooking the street, but Lady Daphne had bragged all those years ago about buying a whole building, one of the tallest in Raleigh at the time, so she must own the hotel as well.

Loud music leaked out of the front door when a muscular woman in a black T-shirt opened it to let people in. The T-shirt said "Mirror" in reflective silver letters, then had the same word beneath it, upside down in gray.

Even this early in the evening, few people came out the doors. Most went in. *A lot* of people went in. The pounding music drew the Normals to dance and intoxicate themselves until they became easy prey. Liliana suspected the nightclub would draw the more predatory beast-kin and Fae, as well as the often equally predatory humans.

Noisy, crowded places like this were why Liliana no longer went dancing.

Another door led into the hotel lobby, but it had nearly as many people pouring in as the door directly into the nightclub. Inside the hotel lobby, her fourth vision showed her another entrance to the club was also guarded by an athletic woman in a black T-shirt.

In a few minutes, Liliana knew Pete and his friend, Sergeant Giovanni, would enter the building. Neither of them would leave it again unless Liliana changed their paths.

It was her fault. She told Pete he should speak to Lady Daphne.

Liliana huddled in the shadowed doorway of the closed offices glaring at the building filled with noise and people and mad flashing lights as if it were a vicious enemy. She absolutely could not walk through that door. She shuddered with revulsion and something like terror thinking about it.

The spider seer had always hated being stared at. And crowds always stared at her. Worse, in a crowd the short spider-kin was often bumped, touched, jostled, and shoved around. If she tried to force herself to go inside, she would instinctively shut down, go to that blank place in her mind where time passed without her awareness.

That would not help Pete.

His life depended on her. Two lives. She liked Sergeant Giovanni too, even though the sergeant still believed Liliana was a charlatan, and possibly still thought she was a murderer.

But even if her own life had depended on it, Liliana could no more walk into that building than she could stroll into a bonfire.

She considered speaking to Pete and Sergeant Giovanni before they entered.

Maybe she could warn them.

Would that save them?

An image of herself appeared before her fourth eyes of Liliana blocking their path on the sidewalk, trying to convince Pete and his friend not to confront Lady Daphne. "You will both die before morning," she told them.

Sergeant Giovanni's eyes narrowed. "Is that a threat?"

"It is not a threat. It is a warning."

Pete put a hand gently on Liliana's shoulder. "We have to find the murderer before they kill again. Even if you're right, and investigating will get us killed, we can't just stop looking. You told me yourself, more people will die."

Liliana closed her fourth eyes.

A warning would change nothing. Duty drove them. They wouldn't shirk that duty, even if it meant their deaths.

If she was going to change things, Liliana had to get in there and do something directly.

She studied the building thwarting her. Brick and windows, balconies and fancy, irregular, decorative architectural features made it look...climbable. The spider-kin could climb a building like that as easily as she could climb a flight of stairs.

A slight smile tugged at her lips, aimed at the building daring to oppose her. She would beat it in her own way.

The Mirror Club and hotel sat at the intersection of two busy streets. An empty, undeveloped lot hid behind it where people parked their cars, and a single-lane alley ran on the fourth side.

To avoid being seen by the woman at the club door, Liliana circled the block, cut through the parking lot, and came at the building from behind. The first two floors were flat brick on this side. Balconies and decorative features started two stories up. Liliana couldn't jump high enough.

A dumpster in the alley solved that problem.

As the spider-kin vaulted to the sheet steel lid of the dumpster, the loud clanging of the steel made her freeze in fear of discovery.

She opened her fourth eyes.

Did anyone hear that?

After a moment of tense searching, she moved again. No one had noticed the noise.

Her new perch made the leap to the lowest balcony achievable, barely, but the angle was bad. The underside of the balcony with its hollow, steel support beams extended over her head, so she couldn't reach the edge to grab onto it. She crouched, gathered her feet under her, and leaped high, right arm outstretched. She slapped the spinneret in her wrist to a balcony support beam. As she fell, a silk line was pulled out. She caught it.

She kicked her legs to swing out and touched the spinneret on her other wrist to the edge of the balcony. As she swung back, a new line pulled out. She grabbed it and let go of the previous line. She popped her arm blade out, swung forward hard to get past the edge of the balcony, twisted, and hooked her arm blade over the edge. The sharp tip dug into the wood decking, allowing her to haul herself up. When her hand closed around the decorative ironwork railing, she grinned to herself, showing her fangs. She would not be defeated by a mere building.

From there, it was a relatively simple matter to stand on top of each railing and leap up to catch the base of the next highest one.

She attached a quick safety line at each level in the unlikely case she missed one of her jumps. Attaching a safety line was habit so ingrained that Liliana's hands did it without her mind having to consciously decide. Every time she actively thought about it, she thought of her first mother.

I always remember, Mut. I won't forget.

Her fourth eyes showed her an image from long past, her first mother smiling and nodding in approval while she dangled from a safety line she had set without being told. Solifu cared far less that she'd made a mistake and lost her footing while practicing a routine on the high wire than that her daughter had developed a habit that could save her life.

Liliana's first mother rarely smiled like that in open approval, far more often stern and disapproving of her mistakes. But while Solifu always pushed her daughter to do better and become greater, the young spider seer's third eyes saw the love and worry in her first mother's aura. And in that moment, approval and relief and love lit Solifu's smile from within with deep blues and rich rose.

As she climbed, a lovely sunset shaded the sky in glowing colors like her mother's soul so many years ago. It made Liliana's smile grow sad, remembering the colors of her first mother's aura that her fourth eyes couldn't look back in time and see.

Each little balcony was equipped with wrought iron chairs and a round, glass-topped table. The furniture looked uncomfortable, but she liked the aesthetics of the curvy strips of metal and thick glass. She scrambled up one railing, around the fifth floor or so, to find a man in a terry cloth robe sitting on one of the chairs, sipping from a mug and reading something on a pocket reader. The devices looked a bit like scrolls with flexible screens that retracted into the cylindrical ends when not in use, but they scrolled out sideways.

Liliana preferred old-fashioned books made of paper, but they were becoming less and less common, and more and more socially frowned upon since the Green Party gained power. The spider-kin liked that the forests grew wild and tall again, but she still guiltily preferred real paper books.

The man on the balcony looked up at her, and his eyes got very large.

Uncertain what was appropriate in this social situation, she waved at the man and gave him her best attempt at a friendly smile.

He waved back, so that was probably the right thing to do.

The spider-kin resumed climbing. At the top floor of the hotel waited a restaurant. She hadn't known that until she pulled herself up and swung a leg over the railing.

A single, very large balcony covered half the area of the building's roof. About a dozen of the pretty glass-topped tables with their accompanying wrought iron chairs sat on the rooftop. The weather was much more pleasant than yesterday, warm and dry with a soft breeze. It looked like a very nice place to have dinner. But she was not hungry, and she needed to figure out how to save Pete and Sergeant Giovanni.

In between a young couple at one table and a man in a business suit sitting by himself at another, Liliana swung her other leg over the railing. Discreetly, she detached her safety line from her wrist behind her back as her ballet slippers settled on the terra-cotta tile.

She waved and smiled. Apparently, it was the polite thing to do. The young couple looked at each other, then waved back. The man in the business suit never looked up from his wrist phone. Liliana shrugged and went on. She wasn't the only one who didn't know how to behave in certain social situations.

Wide, wooden-framed glass French doors, propped open to take advantage of the evening breeze, led her into a large room with more of the same type of tables and chairs and terra-cotta tile floor. The room was filled with people chatting and eating, and servers bringing food and clearing away dishes.

Noise and the pleasant spicy scents of garlic, oregano, and rich coffee washed over her as she entered. A lot of people glanced up at her, making her acutely uncomfortable. She looked down at her feet and smoothed her scarlet skirt with the black waistband and ruffle at the bottom. It matched the scarlet scarf wrapped around her forehead and braided into her hair and her black, short-sleeved top with the red roses embroidered on it.

A server looked at her oddly as he set a drink down on one of the tables.

His forehead wrinkled, then he went back toward a door at the rear of the restaurant. He passed a woman who came through the other side of the swinging door from the other direction carrying a huge tray laden with steaming plates of food. That must be the kitchen.

Liliana only had a few seconds to decide what to do before the server fetched whoever was in authority and sent them over to question her. There were three other doors on the back wall, labeled "Men," "Women," and "Ungendered." The only door on the right wall had a small podium with a stack of menus in front of it. A big sign saying "Please wait to be seated" was tilted so it would be visible to people coming in from that door, and a small sign saying "EXIT" in red letters hung above it.

Since she did not need to use the bathroom or go into the kitchen, she chose the door marked EXIT, even though she did not wish to leave the building she'd just gone to so much trouble to enter.

The spider-kin stepped out into a little foyer. Two elevator doors faced her. Getting into a tiny, enclosed room with strangers and no place to run or hide was not a good option. Liliana's nose wrinkled at the thought. She looked around for an alternative.

Another door had a picture of stairs on it and another red EXIT sign. She ducked through quickly.

As she closed the stairwell door behind her, she heard someone open the restaurant door. Liliana opened her fourth eyes for a quick peek behind to see who followed her. She saw the waiter who had wrinkled his forehead at her and an imposing chubby tower of a woman. She had shiny black hair in a bob just under her chin. She wore an apron dusty with white flour and a pinched look of annoyance. They looked around the empty foyer Liliana had just left, a puzzled frown on the server's face. He started toward the door to the stairwell.

Liliana climbed over the railing, attached a quick safety line to the concrete stairs, and grabbed the edge with her fingertips. She swung her feet up to hook her toes under a stair edge.

The waiter opened the stairwell door just as she snugged her body up flush with the underside of the staircase. The big woman in the apron peered into the stairwell, saw empty stairs, and cocked her head to listen for footsteps.

The spider-kin held her breath.

The elevator dinged. Six people stepped out, laughing and chatting loudly, obviously a bit intoxicated. Instead of pursuing Liliana further, the waiter welcomed the new guests to the restaurant, and the large woman went back to the kitchen.

Liliana sighed in relief.

Okay. She was in the building. Now what?

For want of any better ideas, Liliana followed the stairs down. Several floors were hotel rooms. Those floors required a card key to enter. As she reached ground level, she passed two floors with loud music vibrating through the walls. No card key was needed on these floors but she still could not bring herself to enter that pandemonium.

The sound insulation between floors was impressive. The pounding music would be unlikely to disturb the hotel guests in their rooms.

She kept going clear to the basement where the stairs stopped, then hesitated, unsure where to go from there.

A door led out of the stairwell and into the basement proper, which was completely quiet compared to the noise of the two floors above.

While she wondered what to do next, a door opened two floors above her. Thumping, cacophonous music flooded the stairwell for a moment. Light footsteps started down, the quick tap, tap, tap of high heels.

Liliana looked around for a place to hide. The stairwell was bare concrete, and she didn't know what waited in the basement.

As the footsteps came closer, the spider-kin ducked into the tiny, unused nook under the bottom of the concrete and steel stairs. She crouched in the dark corner and hoped she wouldn't be seen.

A petite young woman with long blonde hair tapped her high heels down the concrete stairs over Liliana's head. The short skirt of her cerulean-blue dress with the open back swirled around her thighs as she hurried down the stairs.

Liliana admired the pretty dress through the concrete with her fourth eyes.

The young woman opened the door to the basement and went through without showing any sign of noticing the spider-kin crouched under the stairs.

This seemed to be an excellent hiding place.

She was deep inside the building that had seemed impossible to enter, and concealed well enough that even if her visions distracted her, it was unlikely she'd be attacked while vulnerable.

Now came the really hard part.

She took a deep breath to brace herself against the ugly visions. She could do it. She had to.

Where are Sergeant Giovanni and Pete, and when and how will they die?

CHAPTER 12

WOLF'S BANE

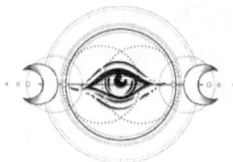

Liliana was immediately assaulted by the same image of Pete's dead face she had seen so many times in the last few hours. Pete's death was so close in time, so close to certain and so horrific, it was nearly impossible for her to see past it to anything else.

Dammit.

She pulled at fistfuls of hair on either side of her head. The spider seer desperately needed her fourth vision to obey her, but it showed her only death, again and again. Not what she needed to see to stop the death from happening.

She hissed with frustration and closed her fourth eyes.

With deep calming breaths, she fought for control of her vision.

It did little good. Every time she looked for Pete, she saw him die. Again.

If she was going to save Pete, she needed to see more than the horror show image of his staring dead face frozen in a silent scream.

Perhaps she should shift her goal.

Just Sergeant Giovanni. What will happen to her?

Warily, she cracked her fourth eyes open, focusing on the human military police sergeant.

Liliana saw a meat cleaver come down and sever the pretty soldier's head while she lay unconscious on a butcher-block table.

The spider seer closed her eyes quickly.

No, she had to look. She couldn't help if she didn't look.

The moment she reopened her fourth eyes, she again saw Zoe Giovanni's death.

Liliana flinched as the cleaver came down but fought her instinct to close her fourth eyes. Sergeant Giovanni's death would at least be less agonizing than Pete's. It would be painless and comparatively peaceful. The spider-kin forced herself to keep watching.

A muscular, dark-skinned woman in a black T-shirt and a chef's apron continued chopping up Sergeant Giovanni's body as if butchering an animal for food. A large plastic can sat nearby labeled "Edible Garbage."

The room was clearly a large, professional kitchen. A door swung open and Lady Daphne Fairchilde herself walked through it. Through the door, Liliana glimpsed a darkened room filled with glass-topped tables. The wrought iron chairs were neatly stacked against one wall. "Well done, Stella. Margaret and I have the car nearly packed, and Kristen should be finished by now. Meet us in the basement once you've disposed of that."

So, Sergeant Giovanni would be killed by a woman named Stella in the restaurant on the top floor, but it would be much later, after the restaurant had closed for the night and all the people were gone.

Lady Daphne was somehow involved in the killings, but Liliana did not understand how or why. Lady Daphne did not sleep with men, so she was highly unlikely to be pregnant. Why would a widow spider kill Other men with her fangs and eat them if she didn't have to? Why would she have one of her employees kill Sergeant Giovanni? The sergeant was neither male nor Other, so she could not nourish unborn widow spider babies. Her death could not help a pregnant widow spider if there was one. What was the point of all this killing?

Liliana followed Lady Daphne backward in time. Having a

different thread to unravel let her go around the vicious image of Pete's death.

What does Lady Daphne have to do with Pete and Sergeant Giovanni's death?

Lady Daphne stood on the second floor of her nightclub near the DJ's booth. A few people danced around them and many more gyrated to the music down on the huge dance floor they overlooked. Mirrors on every wall bounced and magnified the noise, laser lights, and holographs, dazzling and confusing Liliana's inner vision. She blinked repeatedly, but she forced herself to keep watching.

The owner of the hotel and the Mirror Club looked like she was pushing forty, but spider-kin tended toward extremely long life spans, second only to the Sidhe who never aged. Liliana had met Lady Daphne more than eight decades ago, and she'd looked no different then. The widow spider's true age could probably be measured in centuries.

Lady Daphne stood more than six feet tall and weighed well over two hundred fifty pounds. The black velvet corset she wore with her scarlet dress pulled in her ample waist and accentuated her hips and breasts, giving her an hourglass figure. Her shoe-polish-black hair hung to her waist, with bangs cut in a sharp slash across her forehead. Lipstick the color of fresh blood matched her long, perfectly manicured fingernails.

The petite woman in the bright blue dress who Liliana had glimpsed going down the stairs to the basement earlier stood beside Lady Daphne, looking worried. Next to Lady Daphne, the woman in the blue dress looked like a child. She looked barely old enough to drink alcohol legally, and she probably weighed no more than Liliana did. With a wig to change the color of her hair, Liliana could see how she and the girl would match the same descriptions. A small, curved bulge on the pretty young girl's lower belly made Liliana suspect who the murderer Pete sought must be.

A muscular dark-skinned woman wearing the same black and silver Mirror T-shirt as the woman at the door leaned in close to Lady Daphne's ear and shouted softly over the musical din. "An MP and some guy are asking for you by name. What should I do, ma'am?"

Liliana recognized her with a jolt. This was Stella, the woman who would kill Sergeant Giovanni.

Lady Daphne and the young woman looked down at Sergeant Giovanni and Pete as they waited by the bar on the first floor, showing pictures of the missing men to the bartenders and customers.

In a posh British accent, Lady Daphne whisper-shouted in Stella's ear, "Are either of them Other?"

"The man smells canine. I think the woman's a Normal."

"We can't use her in any case," Lady Daphne said. "Get something to take her mind off things for a while and let the others know. Then bring them both to my office."

"Yes, ma'am." The muscular, dark-skinned woman gave the petite woman in the blue dress a reassuring squeeze on the shoulder, then melted back into the crowd.

The petite pregnant woman in the blue dress wrapped a lock of shiny blonde hair around her finger nervously. "The doctor didn't send them," she shouted just loud enough for the woman standing next to her to hear. "He'd have told us."

Lady Daphne petted the young woman's hair gently. "Don't worry about it, love. I'll take care of everything. We shall simply need to leave a bit sooner than we planned."

"I'm sorry I'm causing you so much trouble."

The big woman's scarlet-painted lips thinned, and her eyes narrowed in obvious anger, but her hand on the girl's head stayed gentle. "None of this is your fault, Kristen. The bloody bastard panther-kin who violated you is the only one who did anything wrong. His death was well-earned."

The girl, Kristen, ducked her head, letting her long blonde hair fall forward to hide her face. "Maybe he deserved it, but the other men were innocent."

Lady Daphne made a very unladylike snort. "There's no such thing as an innocent man, my dear girl. And you heard the doctor.

Those men would have died regardless. You simply made use of their bodies." She lifted Kristen's chin with her hand, wiped a tear from her cheek with her thumb, then gave her a quick one-armed hug. "Go on downstairs, love. We'll meet you there in a few minutes."

Kristen nodded and went, just another pretty young college girl in a crowd of hundreds.

So, the girl in the blue dress who had run down the stairs a few minutes earlier was Kristen, and she was a pregnant widow spider. Her nest sisters were feeding her and protecting her. That explained a great deal. Liliana's fourth eyes must be looking at the very recent past.

Liliana wondered who the doctor they talked about was, but she had more important things to focus on right then. If Kristen had already gone downstairs, then time was running out.

When will Lady Daphne meet Sergeant Giovanni and Pete?

Her vision jumped in time. According to the clock on Lady Daphne's desk, she now saw mere minutes into the past.

Stella stood behind Sergeant Giovanni and Pete as they sat in two chairs in a small office. The din of music was muted enough that they could converse normally.

Lady Daphne sat behind the desk. She looked at pictures of the murdered soldiers and shook her head. "I'm terribly sorry. I don't know any of these men."

"One of them was seen at your nightclub," Pete told her.

That wasn't true as far as Liliana knew.

Sergeant Giovanni glanced at him with one eyebrow raised but made no comment.

Perhaps Pete's words were not a true statement but were simply provided as a plausible reason to question a nightclub owner in Raleigh about murder victims found in Fayetteville?

Liliana knew lying was a thing other people often did, but it still disturbed her sense of reality. What was was, and she could no more say it was otherwise than she could unsee a thing that had been seen.

Lady Daphne shrugged. "Hundreds of people come here every

night. Surely I can't be expected to remember all of them." She chose a stylus from the cup full of various decorative styluses on her desk and signed a form on the pocket reader in front of her. Setting the reader to the side, she scrolled out and glanced down at the next one.

Pete chose a stylus from the same cup and played with it idly. The stylus was thick and shiny black with a red hourglass design on the side. "No, but since they were killed by having their dissolved insides sucked out through two large holes in their throats, I thought you might take a special interest."

Lady Daphne's eyebrows went up. "I take it you are aware of my race?"

Pete nodded but didn't add anything. He placed the stylus back in the cup with the others, clearly waiting for Lady Daphne to say more.

"I would be interested to know where you came by this information." Lady Daphne's eyes narrowed, and her lips tightened.

Sergeant Giovanni murmured something under her breath the others didn't hear. "I'd like to know that myself." She leaned forward, put her elbows on Lady Daphne's desk, and said at a normal conversational level, "It's our job to be well-informed about the Others in this state."

Lady Daphne smiled, a show of white teeth. She gestured to her tightly laced black velvet corset. "As you can see, I am most certainly not pregnant..."

Stella snickered.

Lady Daphne continued, her shark smile widening at the shared joke with her employee. "...so if you're implying I killed these men because of the drives of my nature, you need to do your research a bit more thoroughly."

Sergeant Giovanni smiled back at her, showing her own white teeth. "No one is accusing you. We only meant you had a stake in keeping your people's reputation in the community free of allegations. Maybe you could look at those pictures again. Something might ring a bell."

"I assure you none of my people are responsible for this, but I'm delighted to help the authorities in any way I can." Lady Daphne glanced up at the tall, dark woman standing behind them. "Stella, love, do any of these men look familiar to you?" She held the pictures up across the desk.

The muscular woman, Stella, leaned over Sergeant Giovanni, placing a hand on her shoulder as she reached for the pictures.

The sergeant flinched. "Ow."

"Sorry," Stella said. "A drunk broke a bottle over my hand the other night. I haven't gotten my engagement ring repaired yet. It tends to snag on things." She showed Pete and Sergeant Giovanni the metal tine that stuck up next to the central stone on her ring.

"You're engaged?" Pete said. "Congratulations."

"Thanks." Stella favored him with a wide, bright grin.

"I don't suppose you got engaged because you're pregnant?" Pete asked.

Stella barked a laugh. "That would be quite a miracle, sir."

Pete's brows scrunched together for a moment, then widened as he put the pieces together. "Well, congratulations again then."

"Thanks again," she said with a grin.

Carefully, Stella looked at each of the pictures. "Huh. I've seen this guy here a few times. I remember him." She handed the picture to Sergeant Giovanni.

The sergeant's eyes narrowed. "Why do you remember him when Ms. Fairchilde doesn't?"

"He hassles some of the young college girls when he gets drunk." Stella shrugged. "I've had to call him an auto-cab a couple times."

Sergeant Giovanni looked at the picture. "Corporal Araus, right." She probably wasn't even aware her lip made a slight sneer of disgust. "When was the last time you remember seeing him?"

"Some time last month, I think. He stuck his hand up the skirt of a girl barely old enough to get in the door." Stella made a face. "You know the type, Sarge."

The MP and the bar bouncer shared a wry expression. "A little too well, unfortunately," Sergeant Giovanni said, then yawned. She shook her head and blinked repeatedly.

Stella leaned forward, placing her ringed hand on Sergeant Giovanni's shoulder. The sergeant flinched again. "Are you all right, ma'am? You don't look so good."

"I...I feel a little..." The sergeant fell forward. Stella caught her before her head could hit the desk and eased her body back into the chair.

Pete jumped to his feet and pulled his gun from the holster under his synth-leather jacket. "Get away from her." He pointed the gun at Stella.

Stella shook her head. "I don't think you want to do that, sir. I gave her two doses of a strong sedative to knock her out quickly." She showed him the hollow tube leading up her sleeve. Her hand with the sharp ring hovered just over Sergeant Giovanni's throat. "Another dose could be fatal."

While Pete's attention was on Stella, Lady Daphne pulled her own gun from a holster mounted under her desk and pointed it at Pete. "Your friend won't be harmed as long as you don't do anything stupid. Place your gun on the desk."

Pete hesitated.

Lady Daphne moved the muzzle of the gun until it pointed at the unconscious sergeant. "Now," she ordered.

A muscle in Pete's jaw tightened. He pointed his gun at the ceiling and raised his other hand. "Just don't hurt Zoe." He laid the gun on the desk.

Without taking her eyes off Pete, Lady Daphne opened a drawer and slid his gun into it. She pushed a button on an intercom. "Leslie, darling, I could use a couple of extra hands with an unruly customer in my office. Family only."

"Yes, ma'am," a feminine voice answered.

"Put the sergeant's handcuffs on yourself, if you please, Mr. Teague," Lady Daphne ordered.

"Zoe didn't bring cuffs with her." Pete gave a shrug.

Stella shook her head. "She's in uniform. I served a couple of tours myself, sir. I know there's not an MP around who doesn't carry cuffs with them when they're in uniform."

Pete tensed as if about to fight, but Stella moved her hand right over the pulse point on Sergeant Giovanni's throat and shook her head. "I wouldn't if I were you, sir."

Pete pulled Sergeant Giovanni's cuffs out of the nylon case on her belt by her right hip. He locked them loosely around his own wrists in front of his body.

Stella kept one hand over Sergeant Giovanni's throat and squeezed the cuffs with the other, ratcheting them down tight around Pete's wrists until he winced.

Two more athletic women came in through the office door, letting in the noise from the nightclub. Through the door, Liliana glimpsed a corridor of one-way glass with people dancing on the other side, oblivious to what was happening a few feet away. "Stella, take the sergeant somewhere more comfortable," Lady Daphne ordered. She came around the desk, gun pointed at the red wolf. With the other hand, she picked up the black pen with the red hourglass design Pete had played with earlier.

"No!" Pete growled. "She stays with me." He turned his back on Lady Daphne to reach cuffed hands out to grab Stella's arm.

Lady Daphne placed her gun against the back of his head. "Your opinion was not requested."

"You're not going to shoot me," Pete said, ignoring the barrel pressed to the back of his neck. "You need me alive."

Lady Daphne chuckled. "You're quite right, of course." Behind his back, she bit and twisted the cap off the stylus, exposing a needle. She inserted the needle into his neck and pushed the back down before he could realize his danger. "You are needed alive, but I believe unconscious would be better for all parties involved."

Pete tried to hit Lady Daphne with an elbow, but she neatly stepped back out of reach. As the wolf-kin dropped to one knee and fought to stay awake, Stella patted him on the shoulder. "It's better this way, sir."

The sound of three sets of heavy feet coming down the stairs over her interrupted Liliana's visions. It was Lady Daphne, Stella, and another woman, Leslie most likely. They carried Pete between them.

Liliana tensed in a quivering crouch, wanting so badly to attack them. They had Pete. They were going to kill him. He would die screaming if she did not stop them. Her fourth eyes popped open against her will and assaulted her with visions of her own blood splattered all over the stairwell. Attacking right now would be a supremely bad idea. She couldn't save anyone if she was dead.

The spider-kin huddled into her dark corner under the stairs until they passed through the door into the basement. Liliana was a fierce warrior, the daughter of three warriors, trained from childhood to fight, but she was not certain she could defeat a single widow spider in fair face-to-face combat, much less an entire nest of them. Liliana had no idea how many of the women who worked for Lady Daphne were spider-kin, but based on widow spider tendencies to live in nests of their own kind, probably most of them were.

Sergeant Giovanni and Pete's lives depended on her, but Liliana was outnumbered and outmatched. If she did nothing, they would die. If she did the wrong thing, they would still die, and she would die with them.

She had one advantage over other spider-kin: her eyes. There had to be a moment coming up soon when she had a chance to save Pete. Sergeant Giovanni would live for a few hours yet, but Pete's helpless body was being carried straight to Kristen, the pregnant widow spider. Liliana dove back into the vision of her fourth eyes and searched forward in time frantically.

How can I save Pete? When is a moment when I might have a chance?

The vision of Pete's dead face overwhelmed her again, but she tried to fight past it with slow, deep breaths. She needed to see what happened in the time just before he died. She had to see when she could save him.

She still couldn't see anything but his death.

Stella. I need to see what Stella will do in the near future.

That did it. She was able to watch what would lead up to Pete's death.

And Kristen, what will she do soon?

With a thrill of trepidation, she found the moment she so desperately needed. It would not be easy for her. It would be terrifying and painful for Pete. But if she acted at the wrong moment, he would die and so would she.

The odds were not good that she would succeed any way she looked at it.

As Liliana watched and did nothing, Stella and Leslie removed their black T-shirts and shifted to demi-spider form. The hair on their heads withdrew into them as if growing in reverse. Their skin hardened into chiton like lacquered metal, Stella in shiny black and Leslie in brown with bands of black around her joints, both with distinctive red hourglass markings on their stomachs. Four extra limbs emerged from their backs with barbed, wickedly pointed tips, Leslie's with black knee joints. With those pointed limbs, they pulled silk from spinnerets at the base of their spines just above their belt lines. They easily lifted and moved the over two-hundred-pound wolf-kin.

They took the knives from the sheaths he had hidden on his wrists and shins, back and belt, and tossed them to the side.

Liliana sat in her corner in the dark under the stairs and waited with all but her fourth eyes closed. With her fourth eyes, she watched what was happening on the other side of the basement door now in current time. The three formidable widow spiders bound Pete thoroughly in silk.

Pete weakly struggled against the spider women, even as they wound his body with more and more layers.

"He's waking up!" Leslie commented, in a voice like the squeak of an old rocking chair.

"Impossible. It's far too soon," Lady Daphne, still in her human form, said. "I gave him enough to knock out a wolf-kin for hours."

Stella looked up at her boss with bottle-green, faceted eyes in a face out of a nightmare. "He has red hair," she creaked around large fangs. "Maybe he's a Celtic wolf? I've heard they're stronger."

Lady Daphne seemed pleased at that idea. "Excellent. He will provide greater nutrition for the babes than an ordinary wolf-kin. Wrap him with double the normal amount of silk."

"Yes, ma'am."

Kristen, the pregnant widow spider, waited for them to make her prey helpless, tears in her eyes. "You said he would be unconscious. He wouldn't feel anything."

"He is stronger than I knew, child," Lady Daphne told her. "But this will benefit your babies. You must be strong for them."

Kristen sniffed and lifted her chin, her hand stroking her swollen belly.

Pete's eyes opened wide, adrenaline jolting him to a muzzy wakefulness as the pretty young woman shifted form. Her skin hardened and darkened to the dark brown of shiny leather shoes. Fangs as long and thick as a tiger's emerged from her hardened lips and dripped a viscous fluid. Where a drop fell on the concrete, it sizzled and smoked. Four extra insectoid limbs with barbed stabbing tips and black knees sprouted from her back. The pretty blue dress she wore left her back exposed, allowing the extra limbs to move freely.

Liliana rocked back and forth and twisted the silken fabric of her red skirt in knots. She did not want to see this. She did not want to be here.

But she waited. She had to wait. She had to.

Pete's scream echoed on the concrete walls of the stairwell.

Liliana covered her ears and buried her face in her knees.

CHAPTER 13

BINDING NEGOTIATIONS

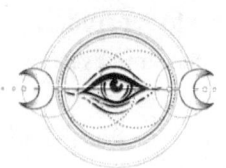

LADY DAPHNE, STELLA, AND LESLIE WALKED UP THE stairs a few minutes later, talking about plans to disappear to other parts of the world.

"Give everyone a bonus tonight when they complete their shifts," Lady Daphne said. "Divide everything left in the safe evenly, then advise our sisters to hastily go their separate ways. We can meet again in a few months in…Texas, I think. I hear Austin is nice. I own a building there under one of my pseudonyms. I shall transport Kristen after she has fed. Stella, you and Margaret meet me in the restaurant kitchen an hour after closing."

"What about the MP?" Stella asked.

Their voices were swallowed by pounding bass music as they opened the second-floor door and left the stairwell.

Liliana didn't bother to follow them with her fourth eyes. She knew what they would do to Sergeant Giovanni. The spider seer knew when and where Zoe Giovanni would die, and had some ideas about how to save the soldier, if she could manage to survive that long. Right now, she had to try to save Pete.

The one moment when she had a slight chance to save him and not die had come.

She opened the door to the basement as quietly as she could and slipped inside. A wedge-shaped hunk of brick sat beside the entrance. Liliana slipped it carefully under the door to keep it from closing with a click and warning her prey.

The scent of damp stone and old blood clung to the cinder blocks and concrete along with a hint of something sharply acrid. Pipes and ducts ran everywhere, but the ceiling was more than high enough so Liliana didn't have to duck under any of them. A bare lightbulb spotlighted the center of the room but left the edges in shadow. Two desiccated bodies in Army uniforms and webbing were stacked carelessly in the back corner. The shadows hid the details of their faces. Liliana carefully did not look. They were undoubtedly the other two missing soldiers, but Pete could confirm their identity later. The last thing she needed was more visions of horrific death right now.

She inched along the bare cinder block wall.

Pete sat propped against the opposite wall in a sitting position, his body completely encased in webbing. Only his head and neck were free. Two fat holes in the corded muscles of his neck oozed dark, thick blood, staining the white webbing. His neck had an ugly greenish color, and crooked branching lines of darker green radiated from the punctures down under the webbing and up onto his cheek.

He coughed wetly.

Kristen knelt in front of him, back in her human form, her arms around her body as if hugging herself. "I'm sorry, I'm sorry, I'm sorry," she murmured like a litany as she waited for her venom to do its grisly work.

Liliana's first mother taught her about the effects of widow spider venom. Pete must already feel as if his veins were on fire and his throat filled with hot coals. In less than an hour, the young widow spider would begin to drink his liquefied insides while he still lived, unable to even scream.

Pete's normally pale blue eyes were dark, his pupils blown wide. His freckles stood out starkly against a face gone paper white with a sickly green tinge. He coughed again and cleared his throat as

Liliana tiptoed from the shadowed edges of the concrete room. He spoke to Kristen, the pregnant widow spider. "Look, it's going to be okay. Just..." He swallowed. "Cut me loose, and it will be all right." His roughened voice sounded calm, soothing.

Liliana looked with her third eyes to see if he were truly that unconcerned.

He was not.

His calm demeanor masked the neon green glow of abject terror. In his place, she would be rocking in a little ball in a corner. Liliana had not seen anyone show so much courage since before her father's death in battle.

The young widow spider in the pretty blue dress shook her head and laughed a little, although it came out more like a sob. "It's never going to be all right!" she yelled at Pete. "You're not even the last one. So many people have to die because I thought it would be okay to date one guy."

Blue eyes tracked Liliana's stealthy progress for a moment as she edged closer, then Pete deliberately looked away from her. He kept talking to Kristen, keeping her attention on him.

"Okay, I know. It's not all right. I get that," Pete soothed, then coughed hard and spat blood on the concrete. "Look," he said hoarsely. "Just give me one of my knives, and I'll get out of this myself."

Kristen looked up from her hands and shook her head. "It's too late. You'll die now, no matter what. The poison is incurable."

Fear poured off Pete like acid-green fog. He couldn't suppress a shudder. "That's not true?" he rasped.

"I'm sorry. I'm so sorry."

Liliana had been taught stealth by a lion-kin and a jaguar-kin. She grew up with big cats as her playmates and her brothers. Her ballet slippers whispered soundlessly across the concrete floor.

Pete's eyes glanced up at her for a moment as she got within striking range of the pregnant widow spider.

Kristen was too immersed in her misery and guilt to notice the lapse.

Liliana flicked her right wrist. The razor-sharp, curved arm blade slid silently from her arm and locked at a right angle. She struck swiftly, focusing the force of the blow through her entire body to give it power.

Kristen's head came off and rolled across the damp concrete floor, the word "sorry" still forming on her lips.

"So am I, little sister," Liliana said softly. The cut was clean. The young widow spider's death was quick. It was the only mercy Liliana could give her. She blinked a few times to clear tears. None of this had been Kristen's fault, but the killing couldn't be allowed to continue. Especially not if Kristen continuing to live meant Pete had to die. "I am so very sorry."

Liliana pushed the kneeling body to the side, away from Pete. Blood spurted and pooled, steaming in the damp chill of the basement and ruining the pretty blue dress.

Pete's pale eyes widened in shock. A few drops of the young woman's blood dotted his cheek. "Lilly." Pete's voice rasped, and he grimaced in pain.

"Don't speak. Widow spider venom destroys vocal cords first." Liliana dropped to a knee and reached a hand to his face to wipe away the blood.

He flinched, eyes showing white all around. Her third eyes told her green terror still flooded him. He did not see rescue when he looked at her. He saw a different threat, come to add some additional torture to his already guaranteed slow, painful death.

Her swift, silent murder of the pregnant widow spider horrified him, even knowing Kristen had been killing him slowly.

"You told me Daphne was...the right kind of..." Pete's sentence was lost in a wet coughing fit. He spat blood at the end of it. Liliana's third eyes saw an image in his mind of what he meant. Pete thought she had deliberately sent him into a nest of widow spiders seeking prey.

"I didn't know Lady Daphne was a danger to you, or I would never have sent you to her for information," Liliana said. "This is all my fault, and I am very sorry, but it was not intentional."

She reached her hand to his face again.

He nodded slightly and let her fingertips brush the blood off his cheek. She had no reason to lie to him when he was already dying from poison. She could see Pete took comfort from her touch. She watched his aura as a strange sort of peace overcame the glowing green. Fear still filled him, but it was lessened. She had accomplished that much. But she could do more.

"Kristen was wrong. You do not have to die tonight." Liliana had bitten him against his will the first time. Her other choice had been to kill him. She had chosen for him, which was not honorable, but he had not fully understood the situation. Now he could choose for himself whether to accept her venom or die, with full knowledge of both options. This was honorable. "My venom can counteract widow spider venom."

Pete looked at her for a long moment, hope blooming in his heart like a pink flower, but he was confused. He opened his mouth to question her reasons for offering to help him, then he closed it without saying anything and nodded. It didn't matter why. He would take any chance to avoid this awful death.

Liliana hesitated. She owed him full knowledge of one important aspect of her venom's magic before he made the choice. "Each time I share venom with you, our fates will become more closely intertwined."

He coughed, spat more blood, and quirked up one side of his lips in a crooked half-grin showing bloody teeth. "I've seen the alternative," he said. "Bite me."

Liliana knelt beside him and put her arms around his wide shoulders.

Pete leaned into her. His muscular body trembled in her arms. His face still showed no signs of distress, but his body and his aura betrayed his fear and pain.

The sticky widow spider silk felt odd under her hands, familiar and yet not quite right, like an old favorite tune played slightly off-key.

His throat was the only part of Pete exposed.

"This will hurt," Liliana apologized. She could not bite a safer spot, and she didn't dare take the time to bite him like she would a lover, to minimize pain.

Rather than speak, Pete leaned his head to the side and pushed his throat toward her mouth.

Liliana bit carefully in the long strip of muscle that ran from Pete's collarbone up the side of his neck to just under his ear, avoiding the big veins. Her needle-sharp fangs made pinpricks just above the gaping wounds the widow spider's lion-sized fangs had left.

His damp skin smelled of fear sweat and the sickly sweet acidic rot of widow spider venom, but under that was formaldehyde and steel and a hint of wet fur: Pete's scent. Liliana made sure he got a full dose of venom, then tasting the harsh acid in his sweat, bit a little harder to push more.

Pete grunted hoarsely next to her ear. A pained sound, but nothing like the agonized scream she heard earlier when Kristen bit him.

She hugged him as the venom's euphoria burned warm and sunny yellow through him, washing away all pain and fear.

He rested his forehead on her shoulder as his breathing slowed and the trembling eased.

Liliana held him close and rocked him like a sick child.

After a few steady, deep breaths, the tension in Pete's shoulders drained away. "Thanks, Lilly," he whispered. "I keep misunderstanding you." He snuggled more comfortably into her arms. "I can't believe I tried to kill you last night," he said with the unfiltered honesty of her venom. His voice was still raspy, but it no longer held the wet gurgle of blood.

"I can't believe I nearly got you killed tonight."

"Let'sh not do that anymore." Her venom's influence slurred his speech slightly.

"Agreed." Liliana hugged him hard. For a man she had known only two days, this red wolf had become precious to her.

"Could you cut me loosh now?" he asked.

Liliana laughed and felt the relief in it, but they were deep in enemy territory. One wrong step would still end both their lives. Even if they stepped as carefully as her eyes could guide them, they had a strong chance of both dying tonight. "No."

"Um..." Pete pulled back and looked at her. "Why not?" She could see him struggle to make sense through the fog of both her venom and lingering sedative.

"Sergeant Giovanni is sleeping in an office upstairs in the back of the restaurant."

"Soooo..."

"If I cut you free, you will want to go and save her, and you are stronger than I am. I will not be able to stop you."

His lips thinned into a stubborn line. "I'm not leaving Zoe."

Liliana nodded. "I could not save you until after you were bitten. I was here, hiding, but I had to wait or we both would have died."

A deep crease of confusion dug its way between his pale brows.

"I'm sorry I'm not explaining this very well." The euphoric fog of her venom probably did not help Pete make sense of her nonlinear thoughts. "I wanted to save you before, but the widow spiders would have killed me, and you would still be dying now."

"Wait, I think I've got this," Pete said with the overly serious air of the very intoxicated. "You're saying we have to wait until the right moment to save Zoe or we'll die trying?"

Liliana nodded.

"And you won't cut me out of these nasty webs because you don't think I'll wait?"

Hoping Pete wouldn't be angry with her, Liliana nodded again.

Pete smiled bright enough to light up the dingy basement. "I speak Lilly!"

She smiled at his T-shirt collar. "Your ability to understand me does seem to be improving."

"Go ahead and cut me loose then," Pete said.

"No."

Pete rolled his eyes and swayed a bit to the side.

Before he could fall over, Liliana caught him. She had given him *a lot* of venom.

"C'mon, Lilly," he wheedled. "I'll wait. I promise. This cocoon thing is sooo disgusting."

Liliana considered. "If you try to save Sergeant Giovanni too soon, then we will certainly die. So will she."

"I got it. I got it. I'll follow your lead and only go after Zoe when you tell me."

"You will do exactly what I tell you to do when I tell you and no sooner," she ordered.

"Aye aye, Cap'n Lilly," Pete said with a grin. "I'd salute, but..." He made a partial shrugging motion under the webbing.

Still, Liliana hesitated. Her venom made people very honest and very suggestible, but when the venom wore off, Pete would do what he willed, and she could not stop the powerful wolf-kin.

"I'm beginning to think this turns you on or something," Pete commented cheerfully. "Every time we meet, I get tied up."

Her cheeks flushed with embarrassment, and she frowned. She realized she did rather like having the red wolf within her power. "I did not bind you this time. The widow spiders did."

"So, get me out of this?" Pete gave her deliberately big puppy eyes. "Pleeeease?"

Liliana sighed. She didn't think she could tolerate three hours of intoxicated begging, and he had given his word. "All right."

She extended one of her arm blades.

"That is pure class," Pete commented as she carefully slid the razor-sharp blade under the edge of the silk by his throat. The wolf-kin held completely still. His breathing did not speed up nor did he flinch, even when the flat of a blade sharp enough for him to shave with slid along his skin.

Wondering if he was hiding fear behind a mask again, Liliana looked into him. She was surprised to find there was no fear inside him to hide.

With raised eyebrows and a tilted head, Liliana looked a question at him, her blade against the thin skin of his throat.

"If you wanted me dead, Lilly, I'd already be dead twice over. I trust you." Her venom rendered him incapable of lying. His complete trust was truth, even though only minutes ago he'd feared her. In risking her life to save his, she gained far more than she expected.

Liliana blinked all four currently open eyes. His trust made her feel odd. No one had ever placed so much trust in her. She liked the sensation, but it disturbed her as well. What if she didn't deserve to be trusted? What if she failed and he died?

Her arm blades' primary evolved purpose was cutting spider silk, so the razor edge parted multiple layers of webbing with ease.

She managed not to cut Pete's skin in the process, but his flimsy synth-leather jacket got shredded, and his T-shirt and jeans got a few slices here and there.

"Careful of the boots," he commented when she got to his ankles. "Magnum High-Techs cost a fortune. They're real cow leather."

Liliana accepted the caution and took extra care not to damage the shiny black combat boots. The tip of her blade caught one of the laces though. "I'm sorry," she said as Pete kicked the last of the sticky strands of the cocoon hard away.

He giggled, a bit too high-pitched to be simple amusement.

Liliana didn't think she said anything funny.

"You saved my life, got me out of that nasty crap, and you're apologizing for cutting my shoelace." He chuckled a little more, shuddered, and swallowed, the smile leaving his face abruptly. He cleared his raspy throat. "I feel like I gargled hot shrapnel."

He dug a handcuff key out of a hidden pocket in his boot and freed his hands. "Zoe's cuffs are stronger than normal. Even I can't break them, but she always has me keep spare keys in case she loses hers." Once completely free, he sat cross-legged and ran his hand through his thick red hair. His hand trembled slightly, as the last image she hoped she'd ever see of his close brush with a painful death flashed in his mind.

"My venom will help you heal, but it will take time." Liliana cut the seam at the bottom of her skirt and tore off the black strip of cloth that made the ruffle. She pushed it gently against the swollen, puffy holes on the side of his throat. The punctures she made were small and neat with just a trickle of blood that would quickly stop. The widow spider's punctures were wide and still sluggishly oozed thick blood and greenish neutralized venom.

"I heal fast." He waved her concern away. "How long do we have to wait before we can go after Zoe?"

Liliana licked her lips and looked down at his boots. "You should leave now, so you can get home safely." If she could get him out, then at least one life would be saved.

She remembered seeing a pack of wolfhounds tearing him apart a few months in the future. It horrified her to think of him dying that way, but of all possible deaths, the widow spider's bite was the only one Pete genuinely feared. She did not want the brave wolf to face this enemy again when he had so nearly died in terror and agony. If he must die, she had seen enough of his soul to know he would choose to die fighting, saving the life of an innocent.

She winced as she realized that, thanks to her, he wouldn't live that long even if he made it out of this building tonight. Meeting her had really not done the wolf-kin any favors.

Pete blinked, fighting his way through venom fog and the urge to obey without question. "We come back later for Zoe?"

"I will get Sergeant Giovanni," Liliana said.

Pete shook his head, struggling against her venom's influence. "I thought you said we could get her free together if we waited until the right time?"

Liliana sighed. She let Pete hold the wad of cloth against his neck and sat back on her heels. "I told you if you tried to save her too soon, we would certainly both die, and so would she." She ran her fingers along the frayed hem of her skirt. It could probably be saved if she rehemmed it shorter, or added a different ruffle. "I did not say we would not die if we waited. You should go home now, so the widow spiders won't kill you."

"And you? And Zoe?"

"I might be able to save her and survive." It was truth, barely. Without the red wolf to fight beside her, the visions of Liliana leaving the building with Sergeant Giovanni were flickery and faint, barely within the realm of the possible. The visions of them both dead in various ways were overwhelmingly more solid. She continued to study Pete's boots. If he relaced it, he could still tie the one she had cut. The laces were long.

"You don't sound very sure." Pete put his finger under her chin and brought her face up. The pupils of his eyes were still wide and black from her venom and the other drugs in his system, but his brows were furrowed with concentration. It took a very strong will to fight the venom's suggestibility. "If I help, do you have a better chance?"

Liliana had never wished harder that she was capable of lying. "If you help me to save Sergeant Giovanni, there is a better chance she and I will survive, but the most likely outcome still is we will all three die. One widow spider is a deadly adversary. A nest of them will be virtually impossible to defeat, and I have seen no path for us to save Sergeant Giovanni without fighting at least one of them, probably more. Go, and at least you will not die tonight."

Pete smiled gently at her, and his soul colors shifted to an affectionate pink. "If you had stayed home, you wouldn't be in any danger at all."

"But you and Sergeant Giovanni would have certainly died," Liliana objected. "I could not stay home safe and let that happen if I could help."

Pete gave her a slow, lopsided grin and spread his hands in a shrug.

"Oh."

He would not leave, not even with her venom and his own fear motivating him.

"Okay then," Liliana said. "We will have to wait three hours. I think many of the women who work here are widow spiders. When the night club and the restaurant close, most of them will leave. Lady Daphne and two other widow spiders will stay to kill Sergeant

Giovanni and dispose of her body. Then they will come down here to get Kristen, believing she will be done feeding on you."

Pete shuddered and looked at the headless body lying in its pool of blood. The deep, confused furrow between his brows appeared again. "Uh, I know I'm high as a kite, but I'd swear that body moved a little, just now."

Liliana nodded. "Her unborn babies still live. They will eat their way out of her body eventually."

His already pale face went even more white. His freckles stood out like coal dust in snow. "What kind of babies eat their way out of their dead mother's stomach?"

"Widow spiders. They begin as hundreds of tiny babies inside their mother. The strongest eat the weaker ones when food inside their mother is scarce. The better fed they were, the more of them would have survived until she gave birth. That is why she had to kill male Others and feed on them, even though she did not want to, so her babies would not eat each other. If she did not feed on male Others at all while they grew, they would eat her too."

If anything, Pete looked worse, like he might throw up. "So a bunch of tiny, cute little babies are chewing their way out of their mother's body right now?" Pete rubbed his arms as if they were cold.

Liliana shook her head. "They are in spider form. Widow spider babies must be taught human form when they are a few years old. They generally learn demi-spider form in adolescence. With their mother dead, only three or four of the strongest will survive. They will emerge from her body starving and hunt small animals for food and spend their lives as giant spiders. They will have no one to teach them how to be people." She felt sad for the abandoned babies. There had been no other choice but to kill their mother to protect Pete and prevent a dozen other deaths, but she still felt sad for them.

Pete got up and walked unsteadily to the other side of the basement, as far away from the dead widow spider as possible.

Steadying his wobbly steps, Liliana followed the wolf-kin without question.

He sat down again with his back to the damp cinderblock wall, facing the body on the other side of the room warily. He looked toward the corner where the widow spiders tossed his knives and started an ungainly attempt to get back to his feet.

"I will get them for you," Liliana told him, and he settled back.

While searching for his knives, she found Kristen's head rolled into the same corner. Gently, she laid it beside her body, pushing the long hair away from the blood and closing the staring eyes. It was the best she could do to give the girl some dignity.

The panther-kin who raped Kristen had done so much damage with a single cruel act. So many had died, and there was more blood and death still to come. Ripples of pain would echo from that single dark deed through lifetimes.

Liliana wished others could see as she did, the many ways each act affected the fate of others, the way every life intertwined with the other lives they touched. Maybe if they did, they would take more care.

Or probably not.

Anyone who would rape a young girl on their first date probably didn't care about the damage he did.

To the dead girl, Liliana murmured, "At least he paid for his crime with his life." But it was cold comfort to the young spider-kin lying headless in a pool of her own blood with her orphaned children growing restless inside her.

Eight knives of various lengths lay in the darkened corner. She brought them back to the red wolf.

Pete's eyes showed white around the edges as he stared at the dead widow spider.

Liliana's third eyes saw into him, the dark horror of the basement full of blood, death, and terror, like he was in a living nightmare that he couldn't leave. The knives sliding into place in their sheaths at his ankles and wrists and on his back comforted him somewhat. He felt safer with them, but he touched the empty shoulder holster with longing.

She would have to get his gun back for him.

He did not seem to want her to sit too close, so she left space between them.

After a while, he looked at her strangely. "Um, Lilly, don't take this the wrong way, but are you likely to get pregnant any time soon?"

Liliana felt her face flush. "I am not yet adult, so I cannot become pregnant for four more years."

He blinked. "How old are you?"

"One hundred and forty-six." Wasn't there some sort of social rule about not asking a woman's age? Liliana suspected the venom made Pete forget that rule.

"You're more than a hundred years old?" he said, incredulously. "If I were a bar bouncer, I'd card you."

Liliana shrugged. "Spider-kin live a long time. My sister, Isabella, is nearly three hundred fifty and passes for a human in her mid-twenties."

"I didn't know anybody but Fae lived that long."

They sat in silence for a while, watching the shadows move over the swollen belly of the headless dead girl.

"So, if you do get pregnant, will it be like, um…will you have to um…" Pete trailed off and gestured to the body.

"Spider seers are the opposite of widow spiders in many ways. We are born completely human and become more and more spiderlike as we mature. I got my arm blades when I was five, my second eyes at ten, my third eyes at fifteen. My fourth eyes didn't open until I was twenty, but that is still childhood for a spider seer. The first time I become pregnant, I will become fully human again for a time, and I should learn how to take human form at will afterward. I should learn full spider form some time in the next century after that."

"So, right now, you can't be totally human or totally spider? You're stuck in demi-spider form?" It was more confirmation than question.

Liliana nodded.

"Will you have a whole bunch of babies like that?"

"I will bear a single spider seer girl child if the child is conceived during the blood-fire time, a boy child of the father's race any other time."

"The father's race? Isn't that usually the same as yours?"

"There are no male spider-kin. We can mate with any Other, or even Normals, although that is rare. Spider seers seek mates who are fierce and strong, who can protect us when we are pregnant and less able to defend ourselves. One of my aunts married Genghis Khan. My father was lion-kin. My sister's husband is Komodo dragon-kin."

"What's the blood-fire time?" Pete seemed less nervous now, just curious.

Liliana shifted uncomfortably on the concrete. "It is a time of... of...intense sexual desire, to the point of madness." She picked a loose thread on the torn edge of her skirt until it unraveled. The idea of losing all inhibitions, even for a short time, disturbed her deeply. To her, losing control of her thoughts and actions equaled insanity, and maintaining her sanity had been the hardest battle of her life when she was younger. Her first mother, Solifu, had to kill the daughter she'd had between Isabella and Liliana. She never spoke of it, and neither did Isabella, but Liliana had seen her lost sister and the events leading to her mother making the choice to end the young spiderling's life. A spider seer whose visions drove her mad became deadly dangerous. It was oddly comforting to know that, as much as her first mother loved her, Solifu would kill her rather than let her become a danger to everyone around her. Now she was on her own. There was only Liliana to make sure Liliana stayed sane.

"I have four years to choose a mate, or my body will force me to choose the nearest fierce male." Liliana's cheeks were very warm. Hormones would override her ability to choose and her honor. She would use her venom to make any nearby suitable male mate with her if she had no obvious mate by then.

Pete didn't say anything for a while, watching the dead woman.

She didn't dare look into him with her third eyes right then. The last thing she wanted to see in Pete's aura was the kind of horrified disgust he felt for the widow spiders. But his silence told her volumes. She had only just managed to make a friend, and now hormonal realities she could not control had made her monstrous in his eyes.

"If we live that long, I will warn you so you can stay away," Liliana almost whispered, human and third eyes focusing on her fingers as they systematically unraveled her skirt edge.

Pete turned to her, eyebrows lifted. He scooted closer to her, closing the distance she left between them. "No, Lilly, it's okay." He put an arm around her shoulders and gave her a squeeze probably meant to be comforting. It was a bit painful, since her venom still interfered with his motor control and he was really strong, even in human form.

"You won't need to warn me away," he said, raspy voice gentle.

Liliana firmly closed her third eyes, then looked up and met his eyes with her human ones for a moment. A trickle of hope filled her chest. She risked looking into him with her third eyes again. She did not see passion. She saw a deep relief that her reproductive cycle bore little resemblance to a widow spider's, and beyond that, affection and gratitude.

Pete did not desire her. She already knew this and respected his loyalty to his beloved. It should not feel disappointing. "Why won't I need to warn you?"

"Because by then, you will have found someone."

"You can't see the future." His arm felt warm and heavy around her shoulders and a bit sticky from widow spider web residue.

"No, but I can see you. You're beautiful and brave, and any man would be lucky to have you." Pete believed what he said, that Liliana would find a mate before blood-fire madness chose some random fierce male for her.

He squeezed her shoulders again and patted her arm reassuringly if a bit clumsily.

Pete had more faith in her ability to find a true mate than she did.

Liliana recognized where she excelled and where she did not.

She was very good at fighting and seeing. She was not very good at relationships and social interaction. She didn't even have any friends —except now she had Pete. The likelihood that in the next four years she would find a fierce, handsome, brave, passionate man and convince this miracle man to choose her for forever was very, very low. She did not need her fourth eyes to tell her that. In fact, she very carefully did not look.

The one hard lesson she'd learned, the one lesson she tried to teach to all her clients, was never to ask a question if you really did not want to know the answer.

Oddly, she thought of the obsidian Sidhe prince, Colonel Bennet, for a moment. No one could say he wasn't fierce, and she found him intriguing. But a Sidhe would be far more likely to treat her as a threat than a potential mate.

"We have nearly three hours before we can try to save Sergeant Giovanni," she said. "You have a strong sedative, widow spider venom, and spider seer venom all in your body and deep puncture wounds on your throat. You need to heal. You should sleep."

Pete looked over at the dead body and scratched at his arms. "Yeah, I don't think I'll be doing any sleeping in here."

"I will keep you safe, Pete." His eyes still had wide pupils and a slightly unfocused look, so her venom still affected how easily he would take orders. "Lay down and go to sleep right now."

"Okay." He stretched out long legs on the cold concrete and used his shredded jacket as a pillow. He fell asleep almost immediately. When Pete had no real objection to her suggestions, his resistance to them was no stronger than anyone else's.

Liliana stroked his thick red hair gently, threading out remnants of webbing and wishing she had some oil. "I will keep you safe," she whispered. She was not certain it was truth, but she was determined to do her best to make it truth.

For lack of anything else to do, she relaced Pete's boot, thinking about the fight to come. His overly large boots made him seem clumsy in human form, but they would be very useful when he shifted to demi-wolf form and his feet, along with the rest of him, got much bigger.

The rest of his clothing was the same. It either fit loosely or was designed to stretch. Even the straps of the knife sheaths tucked into his boots and around his wrists were designed to adjust size with him as he changed shape. Clever. The wolf-kin could take demi-wolf form and return without damage to his clothes. Only full-wolf form would necessitate removing them.

While her hands busied themselves with his boot laces, her mind worried at the problems ahead. Perhaps there was some way to increase the odds in their favor in the fight to come. She searched her mind and the paths of the near future, seeking a path that would lead to Liliana, the red wolf, and the nice Army sergeant all walking out of this building alive.

She did not find one.

Chapter 14

Stella

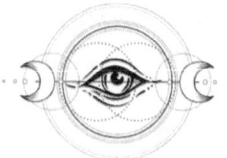

Above them, Liliana watched as the nightclub and restaurant closed for the night. The raucous music went silent. The innocent hotel guests settled snugly in their beds. Most of the employees left.

Only three widow spiders remained: Lady Daphne, Stella, and Margaret, who Liliana discovered was the large woman in the flour-dusted apron from the restaurant.

Liliana walked over to the dead body of the young spider-kin she'd killed. The slightly swollen belly of the headless corpse moved subtly. Her second eyes could see the warm living cluster of spider-kin babies, growing restless as their mother's body cooled. She put her hand gently on the dead woman's belly and blinked tears. "I am so very sorry," she whispered.

Sad and without hope, she sat back down next to her wolf-kin friend. Kristen's life had been the price paid for Pete to survive, but it was a bad bargain if she could not find a safe way for him to survive the night. She had neither thought of nor seen any way to improve their chances beyond the tiniest of unlikely flickers.

Needing some comfort in the cold, dank basement filled with the scent of blood and death, she lifted the head of the sleeping wolf-kin off his makeshift pillow and laid it in her lap.

Pete curled around her legs in his sleep and muttered, "A few more minutes, Ben."

She petted his thick red hair absently while she considered her options. They would simply have to fight as best they could and hope beyond reason they beat the odds.

Pete's destroyed jacket lay under her legs now. Something hard in it poked at the bottom of her leg. She reached into the tattered folds and found Pete's outdated pocket phone. She turned the phone over in her hand.

Wrist phones had electronics built into the wrist band, sensors and such. The wolf-kin had probably not found a way to get one to flex with his size changes like all his other clothing.

She placed his thumb on the sensor pad to activate the phone. She looked over Pete's contacts. Doctor Nudd's number met her eye. Pete trusted Doctor Nudd with his life.

Oh. Pete has allies!

Why hadn't she thought of this before? Unlike her, he had other friends who might be willing to fight at his side.

She touched Doctor Nudd's name in the list to call him.

"What now, Pete?" Nudd's gruff voice answered after several rings.

"I am not Pete. I am Liliana." She kept her voice soft so as not to wake the sleeping wolf-kin. She looked backward in time to see how Pete used the phone. *Oh.* She touched a small image resembling an old-fashioned video recorder. A tiny, poorly lit image of herself appeared in one corner of the screen. The rest of the screen filled with a flat image of the tall goblin.

It seemed likely she had woken Doctor Nudd. It was a bit past three in the morning. He sat in a bed big enough for Liliana and three other normal-sized people to sleep in comfortably. A single lamp beside the bed lit the goblin's messy hair and grizzled face. "Is he in trouble again?" Doctor Nudd asked.

"Pete is safe for the moment, but Sergeant Giovanni is still in danger, and we will both be in very great danger soon, when we go to help her."

"How can I help?" He rubbed at his face. He wore an old-fashioned flannel sleep shirt. She wondered if his bedroom was cold at night.

She opened her fourth eyes to look around Doctor Nudd's room where the phone camera didn't reach. He kept his window open at night. Sheer curtains blew in the light breeze. "I do not know how you can help. I only know we are highly likely to die without aid."

Liliana gave a general outline of their situation to the unseelie healer.

He became more and more agitated as she spoke. "You should have called me sooner," he shouted at her, pacing next to his bed. "Even the mag lev train won't be fast enough to get me from Fayetteville to Raleigh in time to matter."

Guilt and frustration flooded Liliana. "I did not think of it sooner." She was so used to doing everything alone.

Doctor Nudd sighed. "Nothing to be done about it." He scratched at the wiry brown whiskers on his unshaven chin. "I'll see what I can manage. Watch Pete's back, would you? The boy is too brave for his own good, if you know what I mean."

Liliana smiled fondly at the sleeping red wolf. "I do know what you mean."

It was time, but she hated to wake Pete. Sergeant Giovanni had less than an hour to live. If they moved now, there was at least a chance they could save her, and their probability of living was the highest right now.

Rather than putting it back in his shredded and useless jacket, she put Pete's phone in the pocket of his blue jeans. She shook him gently.

"Huh?" Pete sat up with a huge jaw-cracking yawn and rubbed at his eyes. The wounds on his neck were closed, and even in the shadows of the single light bulb, his pale skin had better color.

Her venom had granted him a few hours of pleasant, healing sleep free of ugly dreams, despite his recent circumstances.

Considering her advice nearly got him killed in the most horrible way possible, she was glad she'd at least been able to give him that.

"It is time, Pete." Liliana got to her feet. "Follow me and be as quiet as you can."

He nodded, yawned again, and followed on her heels.

Liliana was relieved to see he planned to keep his word to follow her lead, even now that her venom's influence had worn off. She smiled a little in spite of their dire situation. He gave precise oaths because he kept them.

They crept up the stairs. The pounding bass no longer vibrated into the stairwell. It left everything eerily silent. Liliana opened the door leading to the first floor of the empty nightclub.

The stairwell opened into a narrow corridor behind one-way glass. On one side of the hall, she could look out through the glass to the darkened dance floor. On the other side, a line of doors led to offices and storage areas.

Liliana knew which office door was the right one, but when she turned the handle, it didn't move. Locked.

She stood looking at it for a moment, uncertain what to do. She couldn't break the sturdy wooden door. The knob was made of solid steel. Her arm blades couldn't cut through steel.

Pete raised his eyebrows at her in question.

"Your gun is in there," she whispered.

He shrugged his shoulders, reaching outward with his arms as if to embrace her and four other people. His arms and shoulders lengthened as he did. He tilted his head back and opened his mouth as if to yawn again or howl. Fangs pushed past his lips, velvety red-brown fur flowed over his exposed skin, and wiry whiskers pushed out of his upper lip. His nose stretched forward and darkened to a black, shiny, triangular point on the end of a short muzzle. He gained height and breadth, especially in his shoulders, straining the fabric of his formerly loose, stretchy T-shirt with "Keep Calm. I'm the Doctor" written on the front.

Liliana understood that reference. The television show had been around almost as long as she'd been in America. She'd used her fourth eyes to watch it a few times and found it enjoyable.

Deep, ruddy fur with darker brown markings showed through the slits in his clothing where Liliana's arm blades sliced through cloth when she freed him. The massive wolf-kin towered over her petite form. Only Pete's pale blue eyes seemed unaffected by the change. The aggressive scent of canine filled the narrow corridor.

"Sorry," Pete growled softly and ducked his elongated muzzle, as if his demi-wolf form were somehow offensive. He braced a huge, furry shoulder against the door just above the knob and shoved.

The doorframe splintered around the lock, and the door swung open. The sound of wood cracking echoed in the silent corridor, seeming far louder than it probably was.

Pete froze. He glanced at her.

A quick scan with her fourth eyes showed no one had heard the small noise but them. She shook her head to let him know their enemies were not alerted.

As they slipped into the darkened office, Liliana wished her own abilities leaned more toward strength than vision and agility. Strength like that came in handy.

And it was very attractive.

Liliana tapped the metal on the brass desk lamp to turn it on. She watched the play of light on Pete's fur-covered muscles as he prowled around the office, making it seem far smaller than when Liliana saw it before. The black stylus with the needle sticking out sat on the desk where Lady Daphne left it after injecting Pete in the neck.

Pete yanked opened the drawer in Lady Daphne's desk, barely appearing to notice that it was locked. He reclaimed his pistol with the special bullets that were effective against Fae. A very toothy grin showed how pleased he was to have it back. He slipped it into his shoulder holster.

The gun had an extra-large trigger guard, making it accessible to Pete's enlarged, clawed fingers. Very practical. Liliana wondered if it was the work of a certain flower sprite with a passion for customizing weapons.

Liliana turned the desk lamp off again as they left. She led the way up the stairs she'd descended earlier that day. They climbed all the way past the hotel room floors to the top-floor restaurant. While she waited for the best moment in the basement, she'd searched various possibilities. She'd seen herself and Pete die dozens of ways. Many paths branched from this point, but death lay at the end of each turning. Nearly every death she foresaw would happen in the restaurant at the top of these stairs.

She swallowed as she reached the door where the stairs ended.

Liliana could have stayed home today, could have gone on with her quiet life. She chose to be here in the middle of a widow spider nest where she'd murdered one of their own. She chose again to stay and help Pete save Sergeant Giovanni, knowing the price.

She took a breath and sighed, feeling fear fade. This was her choice—perhaps not to survive, but while she breathed, to truly live. If she died tonight, she would die well. Her parents would be proud of her when she saw them again in the next life.

She looked back at the towering wall of masculine muscle and fur following on her heels. Eyes shimmered inhumanly bright in the reflected light of the glowing red EXIT sign.

She would not die alone. She would have a friend at her side.

There were far worse ways to die.

They stepped out of the stairwell and into the little vestibule with the elevators. Everything seemed quiet and dark. Liliana led the way through the restaurant door and past the seating sign. The scent of old grease and faded spices greeted them.

Stars and the city lights of Raleigh both twinkled through the closed glass French doors leading out to the balcony. That dim light shone on the decorative wrought iron, glass-topped tables. The long shadows on the floor looked like the legs of giant black spiders.

Liliana ghosted between the tables, using every ounce of stealth skill she had.

Behind her, the huge shadow of the red wolf followed, nearly as silent in his big combat boots as she was in her ballet slippers. The man understood stealth.

A small sigh escaped her. So few men of any species understood the essentials of stealth.

Figures that he would already be taken.

Brighter light leaked from the cracks around the double kitchen door, reflecting on the terra-cotta tile floor that had been scrubbed clean and shiny.

As they slipped closer to the kitchen, they heard voices.

"She's an MP investigating a string of murders. People will notice when she goes missing," Stella's southern-accented voice pointed out. "We could just tie her up, leave her to be found by the cooks in the morning."

"That would put the police and the military both on our trail immediately, love. Her death purchases us time," said an upper-class English voice that sounded a lot like Lady Daphne but wasn't. "It could be days or even weeks before they trace her disappearance to the Mirror Club if she simply vanishes, especially if no one knows she left Fayetteville."

To see inside the kitchen, Liliana opened her fourth eyes. The surfaces in the large professional kitchen gleamed. Spotless pans with copper bottoms hung from racks above the broad preparation counters and multiburner stoves.

The big, dark-haired woman in the apron, who Liliana had narrowly avoided earlier that day, stood with a meat cleaver in her hand, arguing. Sergeant Giovanni lay unconscious on a butcher-block table with blood grooves around the edge, clearly meant for cutting up large slabs of meat. The shiny, metal garbage pail marked "Edible Garbage" that Liliana saw in her earlier vision stood nearby.

"Is it really worth killing her, just to gain us a little more time to run?" Stella, the athletic, dark-skinned widow spider who'd knocked out Sergeant Giovanni, stood between the unconscious sergeant's helpless form and the large woman with the cleaver. "We can be two states away by morning."

Liliana found herself liking Stella but fought against the urge.

She could not afford to become fond of an enemy she would likely have to kill soon. Rather than listen to the rest of the argument, she jumped forward in time to the moment when Sergeant Giovanni would die. In her vision of the future, Stella wore the chef's apron and reluctantly wielded the cleaver, killing the helpless detective in the same swift, painless way Liliana had killed Kristen.

The kitchen was empty of any other people. The vision was solid, as certain as any event that hadn't yet come to pass could be. Stella would lose this argument. And she would be alone when she killed the sergeant.

Coming back to the present, Liliana shifted the focus of her fourth eyes.

"Move out of the way, love." Margaret said gently on the other side of the kitchen door. "I'll do what needs doing."

"No. If it has to be done, then I'll do it." Stella sighed. "Just... give me a little time, okay?"

Liliana grabbed Pete's clawed hand and dragged him toward a hiding place. Or tried to. She pulled ineffectually on the mountain of fur and muscle.

Pete's big boots didn't budge. His large ears pointed at the kitchen door. Clearly, he could hear the argument too.

She pulled on his hand again, frantically. Margaret would come out of the kitchen at any moment. If they let her pass, they would have only one enemy to fight. If they stayed here, they would have to fight both widow spiders at once.

Pete shook his head, muzzle swinging from side to side in a stubborn, wordless refusal. He leaned down so he could breathe in Liliana's ear. "They're going to kill Zoe!"

His warm breath tickled Liliana's ear distractingly. They didn't have time to argue. On the other side of the door, Margaret was passing over the cleaver and apron to Stella. They had only seconds. If they fought both widow spiders at once, they would almost certainly die.

Despair hit Liliana hard. If Pete would not follow her lead as he promised, then there was no chance at all they would survive the night. She looked up at the wolf-kin. "You gave me your word," she whispered desperately.

For a moment, the wolf-kin stood there, glaring down at her.

Liliana opened her third eyes and glared right back at the mountain of stubborn red fur and muscle. His warm breath blew on her cheek, smelling faintly of blood and raising distracting goose bumps on her arms.

He turned away and bared his fangs toward the closed kitchen door in a silent snarl as precious seconds ticked away. Walking away from an endangered friend would have been difficult for him in human form. In demi-wolf form, his protective instincts were even more powerful.

Liliana's third eyes gave her a front row seat for the battle raging in the wolf-kin. Her despair deepened. Pete would lose the battle. Such powerful instincts would overwhelm anyone.

But Pete had given his oath.

He shook himself, looked back down at Liliana, and nodded sharply.

No time for Liliana to express her relief or how much Pete impressed her. She just grabbed a clawed finger and ran on silent, slippered feet for the men's room. The closest hiding place.

One side of the double kitchen doors swung open just as they ducked into the bathroom. Margaret walked out of the kitchen while the bathroom door was still shutting behind them. It would make a click sound as it shut that Margaret couldn't fail to notice. She was too far into the room to reach the door, and Pete was in the way.

She inhaled sharply and covered her mouth with her hand to keep the sound from escaping.

Pete saw the direction of her horrified gaze. One long claw hooked the edge of the door just before it would have latched shut, stopping it silently.

Margaret didn't so much as glance in their direction as she walked past.

Liliana noticed an odd smell, like licorice only gaggingly intense.

Little blue cakes of some chemical sat in the urinals beside her. She looked around curiously. She had never been in a men's bathroom before. The social rule against entering the bathroom of another gender was immutable under normal circumstances.

Pete's big ears did a weird sort of embarrassed dip as he saw her looking curiously at the facilities men used for relieving themselves. His ears were remarkably expressive in demi-wolf form.

One of his ears cocked toward the door as Margaret went out to the elevator foyer. The elevator dinged, and the doors opened, then closed.

Liliana peeked with her fourth eyes into the kitchen to see what was happening with Stella and Sergeant Giovanni.

Stella stood some feet away from the butcher-block table, wearing the apron, the cleaver in her hand, watching the soft rise and fall of Sergeant Giovanni's chest.

The widow spider did not want to kill the sergeant. That much was clear. But Liliana had seen that she would anyway. Very soon.

She led Pete back out of the restroom and motioned him to wait behind the kitchen door, where if anyone swung the door on that side open, the door itself would hide him.

She went in. "Killing Sergeant Giovanni will gain you nothing," Liliana said softly, so as not to startle the widow spider too much.

Stella jumped anyway and spun into a balanced fighting crouch on the balls of her feet, the cleaver held high. "Who are you?"

Opening all her eyes and exposing her fangs, Liliana popped out her arm blades. "A sister." She did not have long to bargain, but she didn't want to kill Stella if there was a chance they could end this confrontation peacefully.

"Seer," Stella said. "I thought your kind were extinct."

Liliana shrugged. "The report of my death was an exaggeration," she quoted.

"Mark Twain." Stella grinned at her. She shifted the cleaver to a better grip. "What the hell are you doing here, seer?"

"Protecting people who matter to me," Liliana answered. "Sergeant Giovanni's superiors know where she went. Kristen is dead, and the man she would have fed on is alive and free. Killing Sergeant Giovanni serves no purpose. Leave now and I give you my word, no one will pursue you or your nest sisters until tomorrow."

The tall widow spider's eyes narrowed. "That wolf couldn't have killed Kristen. We trussed him like a Christmas turkey."

"I killed Kristen. The red wolf is under my protection."

"Is he your mate?"

Pete was not hers in that way, but their fates were entangled as closely now as if they were mates.

"We have shared venom twice," Liliana said. It was as close to a lie as she could manage.

"We didn't know." Stella still wielded the cleaver, but her voice held genuine remorse. Even a widow spider would not kill another spider's mate. She might kill her own mate, but not another woman's. Widow spiders had their own sort of honor.

Liliana nodded. "I did not blame Kristen for doing what she must for her unborn. Her death was quick and painless. Nor do I blame you for protecting your nest sister. But I cannot allow you to kill Sergeant Giovanni. Killing her will gain you nothing in any case."

Stella considered her words. Liliana's third eyes showed her she was getting through, then a sudden thought hardened Stella's dark face into anger. "Did you hurt anyone else?"

"Margaret is unharmed," Liliana hastily reassured her.

Stella's relief showed strongly, both in her mind and in a relaxing of her shoulders.

"I harmed no one but Kristen," Liliana added. "And her only because I had to. Even her babies still live. You and Margaret could raise them as your own perhaps?" That would be a very good outcome. The orphaned babies would have new parents, and Liliana and Pete would have two fewer widow spiders to fight.

Liliana opened the door Pete hid behind and held it there, a clear path for Stella to leave.

If Stella left, she would never know Pete had been there. If she attacked Liliana, she would find herself fighting both a spider-kin and a Celtic wolf-kin. Surprise was an excellent strategic advantage.

"Go quickly. Leave town tonight," Liliana instructed the widow spider. Stella was a formidable enemy. She had seen several paths where Stella killed Liliana. If the fierce widow spider left without fighting, Liliana and Pete's chances of survival went up drastically. Also, Liliana did not wish to kill her. The widow spider had acted honorably for her species in an impossible no-win situation. She'd shown mercy and compassion.

Liliana kept her arm blades out though. She had seen before she left the basement that many paths branched from here, some of which led to Stella attacking her.

Everything was in flux now, uncertain, shifting. Liliana's fourth eyes were largely useless now that she'd begun to act, to change what she saw before. From here forward, she could only act with honor and strategy, and hope for the best.

Stella stood undecided for a moment. She looked back at Sergeant Giovanni's sleeping form, and Liliana tensed to leap. She felt confident she could jump onto the widow spider's back before Stella could get to the butcher-block table, but if Stella chose to throw the meat cleaver, all bets were off.

The tall, dark-skinned widow spider looked at Liliana and nodded. "I served with people like her. I'm glad she doesn't have to die." She opened the other half of the double doors and walked warily past the tense spider seer, as far from her as the doorway would allow. Each was ready to fight at any moment if the other didn't keep the uneasy truce.

As soon as she passed through the door, Stella paused just out of reach of Liliana's blades and gave a sort of salute with the cleaver. "Thanks for giving me another option."

Liliana nodded acknowledgment. "I am sorry for the loss of your nest sister." Kristen and Stella were probably not blood kin, but all the widow spiders in a single nest were considered family.

"Kristen was a good kid, but she was never much of a fighter." Stella's face showed a bitter sadness that let Liliana see the centuries-old soul beneath the widow spider's young face. "The world is rarely kind to innocents."

"That is an unfortunate truth," Liliana agreed.

Stella disappeared through the door into the foyer with the stairs and the elevators.

Liliana's arm blades suddenly felt heavy as she breathed a sigh of relief. Maybe they would survive this night after all.

CHAPTER 15

WIDOW SPIDERS

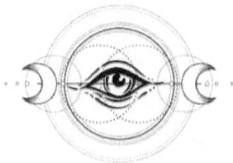

PETE RUSHED PAST LILIANA INTO THE KITCHEN. WITH two clawed fingers on her throat, he checked Sergeant Giovanni's pulse. His huge, furry shoulders sagged with relief. She slept peacefully, unaware of her danger.

The wolf-kin lifted his human friend easily in his arms. He turned and headed for the door.

Liliana shook her head. "No, hide her in the pantry. She will be safer."

Tall, pointed ears laid back against Pete's skull. "We need to get her out of here." His voice was an octave deeper than usual, and gruffer. He sounded as if the widow spider venom had damaged his vocal cords again and he was speaking from the bottom of a well.

Liliana shook her head and stood in the kitchen doorway, blocking his path.

His mind flooded with angry orange, with streaks of clear, light blue protectiveness, like lightning at sunset.

"We are not out of danger, Pete. It will be harder to fight while carrying Sergeant Giovanni."

Pete growled and held the sergeant's body closer.

The spider-kin placed a hand on the soft red fur covering his hard bicep and forced herself to look up for a moment to meet his eyes. "If we win, we can come back for her. If we die, she may still survive if the widow spiders do not find her."

He turned around with a begrudging growl and stomped to the pantry at the back of the kitchen, carrying the unconscious sergeant.

Liliana was amazed again at how the red wolf kept his word to follow her lead, even to the point of acting counter to his own strongest instincts. "Why do you keep trusting me?"

After he laid Sergeant Giovanni gently on the floor next to shelves full of canned food, and stacked bags of flour and dried beans in front of her, Pete growled, "You saved my life and kept Zoe from getting chopped into Zoe steaks." He took a deep breath, and his voice lost some of its gruffness. He pushed stray strands of the soldier's long brown hair away from her face with a careful claw. Then he stood, rolled his broad hairy shoulders, and his ears slowly came up.

With her third eyes, Liliana watched the last of his orange anger fade away. He winked a large pale blue eye at her. "Trusting you seems to be the smart way to go."

Warm cheeks and a twist in her chest happened at the same time, confusing her. His complete trust in her felt good, but it made that awful feeling that she would fail him that much harsher. "Lady Daphne will be here very soon," Liliana said and walked out of the kitchen.

Pete joined her a moment later. "So what's the plan, boss?"

"I will try again to negotiate a peaceful resolution, spider to spider."

"Do you really think that'll work twice?"

"I do not wish to kill if there is any chance at all." Liliana shrugged. "Besides, if we must fight, we will most likely lose. Widow spiders are very formidable."

"They don't seem that dangerous to me now that I'm not drugged and helpless, but I didn't expect going up against you would end with me tied to a tree either. So I'll take your word for it." He grinned at her with a whole lot of teeth.

Liliana found his fierce, canine smile as dazzling as the human version. She stood there and blinked for a few seconds before she remembered where they were. She shook her head to clear it. "If Stella leaves, and Margaret does not deviate from the path she followed when I looked earlier, then we will have about fifteen minutes alone with Lady Daphne before Margaret arrives. We must use those minutes to convince Lady Daphne to withdraw."

"If we kill her as soon as she comes in, we'll have surprise on our side."

Liliana winced. She did not wish to shed the blood of another spider if there was any possibility of a peaceful resolution. Her heart ached for the young girl she already killed, and there had been no other option then. "Hide in the men's room. We will not lose the element of surprise entirely if she believes I am alone."

Pete put a heavy hand on her shoulder. "Lilly, they tried to kill Zoe and me. They've killed a half dozen soldiers. Our chances are better if we kill them quickly."

"Our chances are best if we do not have to fight a widow spider. And there is no more need to stop them to protect others. With Kristen dead, they won't kill anyone else."

Pete sighed and dropped his hand. "Okay, you know what we're up against better than I do."

"If we must fight, kill swiftly and without warning. That is our best chance. But please, wait until there is no other option. Will you promise me you will wait?"

"I'll wait until you give the word," he growled reluctantly.

Just as Pete stepped into the men's room, the elevator dinged in the foyer.

Liliana stood in full view of the entry so Lady Daphne would see her clearly. The door to the men's room was directly to her left. Pete should be able to hear and see a little of what was happening through the inch of space where the door wasn't fully closed.

Lady Daphne Fairchilde walked in with long strides, head high like a queen, red skirt swirling around her knees. She did not seem particularly surprised to see Liliana. "Well, if it isn't the baby seer. I haven't talked to you since we came over on the boat decades ago. What are you doing in my building, little seer?"

"Rescuing my friends. Sergeant Zoe Giovanni and Doctor Peter Teague are under my protection."

Lady Daphne snorted. "You're a little late."

"I am not. I freed them already." Liliana softened her voice. "I am sorry, Lady Daphne. I had to kill Kristen."

Dark eyes snapped with anger. "Kristen was barely twenty, you little bitch."

Liliana bowed an apology, without taking her eyes off her enemy. "I am sorry for your loss. The red wolf was under my protection. I could not permit her to kill him. I had no choice."

"You've got a lot of nerve. What do you think, I'm going to forgive and forget the murder of a young girl in my nest because you apologized?"

"I had hoped you would let us leave peacefully. I have no wish to fight you and yours. Kristen's babies will need someone to raise them." Liliana popped out her arm blades, exposed her fangs, and opened all her eyes for a moment. "There is no need for more blood to be shed between spider-kin." She raised her hands in what would look like a placating gesture to the widow spider but was actually an excellent defensive stance.

With her third eyes open, she could see Lady Daphne's mind flooded with orange anger and yellow-gray contempt. This negotiation was not going well. The widow spider did not fear Liliana at all, and unlike Stella and Kristen, Lady Daphne had no qualms about killing.

The widow spider smiled, and it was not friendly or nice. "Let us leave," she mimicked Liliana. "So, your pets are still here." She glanced at the slightly ajar door to the men's room. "That's very interesting news, isn't it, Margaret, love?" Lady Daphne raised her voice for the last part.

Margaret and Stella came through the door from the foyer. They must have come up the stairs while Liliana spoke to Lady Daphne.

Liliana's shoulders sagged. Three widow spiders at once. The worst possible outcome of all the possibilities she had foreseen. "I let you walk away," she said to Stella, hurt by the betrayal.

Stella had the grace to look embarrassed. "I couldn't go without my fiancée." She reached with the hand without a meat cleaver in it to squeeze Margaret's hand.

The huge woman gave a sweet smile back to Stella.

"And she refused to leave without her sister," Stella said, resigned exasperation in her voice. It was obvious she lost an argument with the other two widow spiders. "Regardless of what happens, I respect what you did." Stella's mind was colored with deep purple-blue regret.

Liliana nodded back. Under other circumstances, she and Stella might have been friends. Now, she would have to kill Stella or die trying. She regretted it and so did Stella. They had their allegiances, and they would each remain loyal to them.

Lady Daphne sneered and rolled her eyes. "Don't play with your food, Stella. It's disgusting." She turned back to Liliana, and her body began to change, growing bigger and harder. "You will pay for Kristen's death, you cheeky little bint. You might as well tell your friend to come out and face me too. It would be so undignified to die while cowering in the gents."

Peaceful resolution was clearly no longer an option. A fair fight with her and Pete on one side and three mature widow spiders on the other was a foregone conclusion. Therefore, fighting fair was also not an option. Pete had promised to hold his fire, to wait for her to give the word. "Pete, don't wait anymore," she murmured. She didn't need to raise her voice for the wolf-kin's tall ears to hear her.

She launched herself at Lady Daphne, arm blades aimed for the widow spider's throat.

Two shots were fired in the same moment, a double-tap. The side of Margaret's head exploded, splattering her fiancée with blood and brains. In human form, widow spiders were as easy to kill as humans.

"NO!" Stella shrieked as if the bullets had pierced her own heart. "No. Not her. Not her." Tears choked her voice, even as her body changed.

Lady Daphne Fairchilde grew four more limbs and a thick black chitinous shell before Liliana finished her leap. Razor-sharp arm blades met steel-hard natural armor, and the armor won.

The widow spider shrieked an inhuman battle cry and tried to bite Liliana's head off with fangs as long as the seer's hand, while the arachnid's massive body kept on growing bigger and bigger.

Lady Daphne's full spider form swelled and towered over the petite seer. Her bulbous body as big as a Volkswagen Beetle stood on ten-foot legs ending in sharp points like pikes. Wickedly hooked claws sprouted along those legs like thorns on a particularly vicious rose stem. Her black velvet corset clung now to the narrow separation between her cephalothorax and abdomen. The skirt of the scarlet dress fluttered like an absurd ruffle around the bulbous black belly decorated with scattered blood red blobs .

The massive creature overturned tables to make room for all that bulk with the deafening crash of shattering glass and iron clanging on tile.

The monstrous spider Lady Daphne had become reared up on her back four legs, showing the well-armored underside of her cephalothorax, and stabbed down at Liliana with all four spearlike front legs at once.

The petite spider seer dodged as many strikes as she could, tumbling like an acrobat. Liliana desperately deflected with her arm blades the blows she couldn't dodge. When even that wasn't enough, she ducked under a table with a heavy glass top and wrought iron frame. Her heart hammered, and she had no trouble at all identifying her own terror.

Spears of steel-hard chiton stabbed down at her. The thick glass cracked in a spiderweb pattern.

Liliana rolled under another table while the nightmare monster shoved the cracked table out of her way.

A creaky hissing squeal of frustration escaped the gigantic black spider.

Two more shots rang out.

Liliana's massive opponent whirled on her many feet to see what happened, ignoring the little seer for the moment.

Pete!

Stella in demi-spider form towered a foot taller than the wolfman. Four jointed, spearlike limbs sticking up from her back curled over her shoulders. The shredded remains of her T-shirt hung like tattered flesh from a heavily armored torso. The cleaver gleamed in a hand armored like a black knight's gauntlet. The blood of her beloved Margaret spattered Stella's shiny black armor in an ugly pattern of scarlet and gray.

Stella didn't flinch as Pete fired three more times. The bullets bounced harmlessly off her chest exoskeleton. She stalked toward Pete, her inhuman face with long, thick fangs made even more terrible by the expression of stark grief on the chitonous face.

Pete abandoned his gun. His bullets ricocheting were more likely to endanger Liliana or Pete himself than their enemies. He launched himself at Stella with a guttural growl, a long knife in one clawed hand.

Like a matador dodging a bull, the widow spider side-stepped his charge and countered his blade with the cleaver. Two of her extra limbs stabbed at him as they circled.

Pete twisted to avoid one of the attacks, dropped his blade to grab her hard, shiny black wrist and one extra limb. He swung her off her feet and around like he was playing airplane with a big kid on a playground.

When the wolf-kin let go, Stella crashed into the stack of chairs along one wall. With a terrible cacophony, the ornate wrought iron chairs fell on her, tangling her long limbs. Liliana hoped the soundproofing on top of the hotel was as good as it was on the lower floors. If it wasn't, they would have curious innocents wandering into the middle of the battle.

Lady Daphne in full arachnid form went up on her front four

legs, using her back four to pull a thick line of silk from her spinneret. She added a loop to the end like a lasso and cast the line toward Pete.

Frantically, Liliana grabbed one of the scrolled ironwork chairs. She yelled, "Pete, duck!" and threw the chair, counting on Pete's trust.

The red wolf dropped to the floor immediately. The chair flew over his head just as the line would have wrapped around his throat like a noose. The lasso hit the chair instead, sticking fast as it flew over Pete.

"Watch for the silk," she shouted.

While the wolf-kin was on his hands and knees, Daphne the giant spider ran toward him. Her sharp feet clacked on the tiles like eight stiletto heels, her fangs dripped thick, green venom.

Liliana jumped up onto a table and launched herself at a shallow angle, careful not to hit the ceiling. She hooked her arm blade under the widow spider's carapace as she flew over it, caught it, and yanked.

The blade, with the full force of Liliana's weight behind it, pulled the giant spider hard enough she staggered to one side just as her fangs struck at Pete, missing his throat by inches and dripping acid venom to smoke on the tile beside him.

Pete scrambled out of the way and up to his feet.

Balancing on the slick black carapace, Liliana lifted her arm blades. Perhaps if she stabbed one of the eyes.

Before she could strike, Lady Daphne let out a piercing, inhuman shriek of rage like the squeal of heavy rusted metal hinges. Her front four legs dropped abruptly, while her back four shoved her body up hard, bucking her unwanted passenger off.

The little spider seer was thrown head over heels right into the glass of the French doors. She curled into a ball and covered her head with her arms and blades as the glass shattered around her.

As she hit the terra-cotta tile of the outside deck, her own weight drove the shattered rain of sharp-edged safety glass gravel into her skin. She rolled to minimize the damage, but when she came to her feet, blood all but coated her. She had a dozen or more cubic chunks of glass embedded in her skin.

She staggered. No bones felt broken, but she made an involuntary sound like a lonely kitten when she took a deep breath. She yanked a piece of broken wooden doorframe as long as a steak knife out of her side. It had skidded on her ribs or she would be dead already. She put her hand over the wound and pushed to slow the bleeding.

She saw Stella fight her way free of the tangle of chairs. The widow spider assessed the situation. Instead of going after Pete, who was still engaged with Lady Daphne's massive arachnid form, she went for Liliana.

Smart tactics.

The spider seer was weakened, wounded, and too far now from her ally to expect aid. She was impressed that Stella could think so clearly, even in her grief.

There was nowhere for her to go. Liliana retreated back between the tables on the balcony.

Stella stalked her carefully, all eight eyes focused on her target. She tossed the tables aside with her extra limbs, overturning them without care.

There was no place for Liliana to run, and no chance of any attack she made having an effect. She watched eight feet of lethal warrior with four jointed spears coming out of her back, shiny black impervious armor, and toxic fangs the length of Liliana's hands get inevitably closer. Stella had no weapons. She must have lost the cleaver when Pete threw her across the room. It didn't matter. The widow spider didn't need weapons.

Liliana hit the edge railing and stopped backing up. She tapped a spinneret to the railing as a safety line out of habit, though there was no such thing as safety right now. She hopped onto the table where the young couple had been dining when she climbed up earlier that day. It meant Stella would have to stab up at her, a less advantageous angle for the bend of her spider legs.

The demi-spider tilted her insectoid head and looked at the little seer with eyes that shimmered with eerie reflected light. Incongruous tears streamed from those inhuman eyes and across the shiny smooth chitin, smearing the spattered blood on her cheeks.

"I am sorry for your loss," Liliana said, feeling strangely sad for the widow spider who was about to kill her. Stella might defeat Liliana, but the widow spider had already lost what mattered most to her.

"You gave us the chance to walk away," Stella said, her voice hoarse and distorted through the fangs. "We could have raised Kristen's daughters together. I just wish..." She drew in a ragged breath and smeared tears and blood across her chitinous cheek with the back of an armored hand. "I wish I could have convinced her to take the chance you gave us."

Liliana nodded, a sadness filling her, not for her own eminent doom, but for the future path Stella had already lost with children and a beloved spouse at her side. Even as she crouched and raised her arm blades in defense, she said, "I wish the same."

"I'm sorry it ended this way," Stella said. She pounced up onto the table with Liliana and grabbed the loose fabric of the smaller spider-kin's homemade blouse. All four sharp limbs struck down at the little seer at once while strong, armored arms kept her from dodging.

Liliana deflected two of the widow spider's thrusts, but she could not deflect the third. The thick claw stabbed clear through her shoulder.

Agony shot through her body like lightning, nearly paralyzing her. She barely felt it as the fourth limb grazed her face, opening her cheek to the bone.

She grabbed the leg stuck in her shoulder out of reflex, then realized she had one chance left to take her enemy with her into death.

The petite spider-kin threw her weight backward with all her remaining strength, hauling the heavier widow spider with her. As she fell, Liliana curled into herself. She pulled her knees to her chin as her back hit the heavy glass tabletop hard. Her fall turned into a sacrifice throw, Liliana continued rolling back, planted her feet in Stella's belly, and shoved with all her strength.

Stella's faceted eyes widened in shock as the widow spider flew for the second time that night, right over the safety railing and into open air. The seams of Liliana's blouse ripped, and it went over with Stella.

The widow spider's hooked claw, still embedded in the smaller spider-kin's shoulder, yanked Liliana's body over the railing as well. She was helpless to stop it.

Liliana let go of Stella's clawed leg and grabbed with both hands the safety line attached to the iron railing.

Stella's weight yanked the widow spider's barbed claw agonizingly out of Liliana's shoulder, wrenching a scream from the seer.

As the arm with the torn shoulder stopped obeying her, the petite spider-kin lost her grip on the safety line with one hand. Blood streamed down her arm and dripped from her fingertips, falling just behind Stella. Down and down a dozen stories into the dark alley and the black unforgiving asphalt. Liliana's right hand held, so only some of her blood followed her enemy down to the ground, not her whole body.

With a crunchy squelching sound, reminding Liliana of that sickening feeling she got when she stepped on a snail in the dark, the widow spider's exoskeleton hit the asphalt.

Stella's mother must not have emphasized the importance of safety lines as much as Liliana's.

Liliana's black blouse fluttered down and covered Stella's shattered skull with embroidered red roses. The seer hung by one arm in her bloody leotard and torn skirt, looking down at the enemy that had so nearly ended her life.

The other woman had been a brave, honorable, and formidable opponent. The widow spider hadn't even screamed as she fell twelve stories. Maybe, in her grief, Stella welcomed death.

"I am sorry too," Liliana said softly. Two deaths of sister spiders now lay heavy on her conscience. Under other circumstances, she would have been proud to name both Stella and Kristen as friends. Her human eyes made hot tears stream down her face from pain of both the body and the heart.

A canine howl of pain and a crash of shattering glass brought Liliana's attention back to her one true friend on the roof above. A guttural growl let her know Pete was still alive. He fought the gigantic spider alone now. And from the sound of that howl, he fought wounded.

Liliana struggled to pull herself hand over hand up the line the mere ten feet she had fallen, but she couldn't. Her left arm screamed in agony when she tried to use it and would not hold any weight. Her bloody hand just slid off the line.

Pete trusted her. He was going to die fighting alone just a few feet away.

Blood and pain flowed in a pulsing river down her arm.

Liliana fought more tears. She had tried so hard to save her only friend. She murdered Stella and Kristen so Pete could live. Meaningless. He would die anyway.

The least she could do was die with him.

She wiped the slick blood off her left wrist onto her leotard to clear her spinneret and attached a loop to her silk line. By putting one foot in the loop and pushing with her leg, she went up a few inches.

A table flew across the railing over her head, passed her on the way down, and shattered in the alley beside Stella's broken body.

By repeating the loop process, Liliana inched her way slowly to the restaurant balcony, wondering as each second ticked past if she would see Pete get hurled across the railing next. She was too afraid to open her fourth eyes and look to see how he fared in the battle above. She could do nothing to change Pete's fate while dangling in the air.

Finally, she rolled over the railing and fell on the tile, panting through the agony in her shoulder that whited out her vision for a moment. When it cleared, she opened her human eyes and dared to look.

Pete was still on his feet, but he had several cuts and stab wounds. Blood soaked his clothing and his ruddy fur.

Liliana marveled through the fog of pain that the red wolf was still standing, still fighting. She had not known anyone so fierce since her father died.

The widow spider faced him, front four legs reared up in attack position, striking down at him as he dodged and growled and hit her with a table frame.

Lady Daphne's exoskeleton showed not even a single scratch. Nothing Pete had done had damaged his opponent in the slightest. Wolf-kin claws and sharp steel knives and even the wrought iron furniture were apparently no more effective against widow spider armor than Liliana's arm blades or Pete's bullets.

Liliana pulled a string of silk from her spinneret and kept pulling, wadding it all into a ball. She stuffed the ball of webbing into the big hole in her shoulder, hoping to slow the bleeding.

As Liliana struggled to her feet, the widow spider stabbed Pete in the thigh. The sharp limb pierced clear through the muscle on the outside of the wolf-kin's leg and stuck out the back.

Pete howled again in agony tinted with battle rage.

"No," Liliana whispered, too exhausted to scream.

Daphne's wickedly barbed leg pulled Pete toward her fangs like a fish on a hook.

Liliana staggered forward, not sure what she could do to save her friend this time.

Rather than fight to pull free, Pete took firm hold of the spider's leg with both clawed hands right up next to where it joined the widow spider's body. He deliberately let his feet go out from under him, falling back until all his weight was on that single spindly limb.

The giant spider staggered sideways, her many legs scrambling to keep from being dragged onto her side by the wolf-kin's weight.

Pete planted his free foot against the underside of the spider's exoskeleton and heaved. His powerful shoulders strained as he pulled and twisted.

Lady Daphne spun frantically in a full circle, trying to shake off the red wolf.

With an ear-splitting shriek of agony, the spider's leg pulled free of the socket. Connective tissue dripping with ichor pulled loose from the widow spider's body along with the severed limb.

Pete dropped on his back in front of Liliana. The seer helped her friend to his feet and pulled him away from their enemy. The severed leg dragged on the tile, leaving a slime trail as Pete staggered backward.

As she screeched in agony, the giant arachnid's seven other legs scrambled madly, knocking tables in every direction. Glass and iron crashed and clattered in a pandemonium to rival the deafening music of the Mirror Club.

Liliana gripped Pete's elbow to steady him as he took hold of the huge spider leg impaled through his thigh. With a hand on either side of an arachnid knee joint, he wrenched backward. It cracked like a giant crab leg. He hefted the thicker part as if considering using the widow spider's armored thigh as a weapon against her. He left the sharp barbed end still sticking through the big muscle in his leg.

He flashed Liliana a fierce toothy grin coated in red from a long gash on the side of his face. Then, his one good leg collapsed.

Liliana tried to keep him from falling, but she could only slow the collapse of his big body to one knee. Him kneeling in his huge wolfman form, and her by some miracle still standing, put them at about the same height.

As they leaned on each other, not sure who held who up, the huge widow spider recovered. Daphne shook herself hard and stood steady on her remaining seven legs. Widow spiders could regrow a lost limb in a few months. For her, it was a minor wound.

The furious spider approached them slowly, wary and limping after her injury. Lady Daphne leaned onto her front three legs with a whine of pain and pulled some silk from the spinneret at the back of her abdomen with the other four. She cast multiple trapping loops in their direction in rapid succession.

Liliana raised her right arm blade, protecting Pete, even though she couldn't lift the other arm. Her razor-sharp blade cut through the silk as it fell. One sticky line got past her and stuck fast to her hip.

Before their enemy could take advantage and pull on the line, one of Pete's long arms snaked out and shredded the silk with his claws.

Pete growled beside her, baring his fangs defiantly at the enemy.

If Lady Daphne wanted to kill them, she would not have the luxury of doing it while they were bound and couldn't resist.

The huge spider paced in front of them, back and forth, looking for the best opening to kill them without taking any more damage. The lost limb didn't slow her down, but she emitted a pained whine periodically.

It didn't matter. All Lady Daphne really had to do was wait for blood loss to weaken them. Well, that was true in Liliana's case. Pete's worst wound was still mostly sealed with the spear of spider claw. Liliana had managed to slow the bleeding from her shoulder with the wad of silk stuffed in the hole, but it still oozed and ran down her arm.

Liliana didn't need her fourth eyes to tell her they were likely to die without even striking another effective blow.

"It was an honor to fight at your side," Liliana said softly.

Pete put a clawed hand covered in blood and ichor companionably on her back. It spanned all the space from shoulder blade to shoulder blade. "Same here," he growled.

Lady Daphne seemed to lose patience in that moment and came for them, fangs dripping with acidic venom, front three legs up high, ready to stab.

Liliana braced herself to meet her death with courage.

Her father and mothers would have been proud of her today.

The BRRRRRAATTTT of a rapid-fire machine pistol halted the giant spider. Bullets sprayed Lady Daphne in the face.

A tortured metallic shriek rang out as three of her eight green-faceted eyes exploded in gouts of sickly yellowish ichor.

Liliana looked behind her. Muzzle flashes exploded with each shot, lighting the rooftop battleground like rapid, red-shaded lightning strikes. They also lit brilliant fuchsia and violet dragonfly wings with a miniature woman in a leather jacket suspended in the air between them. Siobhan's cute pixie face was set in a grim line. Her whole body leaned into the weapon, and her wings beat frantically to fight the kickback.

As the giant spider staggered back, screeching in agony, the tiny Fae landed beside Pete and Liliana.

"Close your eyes and plug your ears!" Siobhan clicked something on her machine pistol and pumped it like a tiny shotgun.

Liliana and Pete did as they were ordered after a confused look at each other and a shrug from the red wolf's hairy shoulders.

Siobhan pulled the trigger. A boom rang out with a recoil that knocked the little Fae onto her butt on the tile.

Through her tightly closed eyelids, Liliana's human eyes were still nearly blinded by the flash, and she was partially deafened by the explosion despite her fingers in her ears.

The ear-splitting screech Lady Daphne emitted didn't help.

"Go for her belly!" Siobhan shouted directly in their ringing ears, then took to the air again. "Nudd said widow spiders have no armor on the underside of the abdomen."

Liliana felt stupid. She had read *The Lord of the Rings*. She should have known that.

With their tiny, well-armed ally on their side, and the new knowledge of the enemy's weakness, this might no longer be a hopeless battle. Pete and Liliana looked at each other for half a second. Pete nodded, and she knew exactly what he would do next without bothering to look into his mind.

The red wolf rolled in a somersault forward and to the left, favoring his injured right leg.

At the same moment, Liliana did the same thing to the right, favoring her injured left shoulder.

They bypassed Lady Daphne's many legs on either side while

Siobhan distracted the spider by spraying the part of her carapace that passed for her face with more bullets.

The widow spider lifted her abdomen and leaned forward on her front three legs so she could pull silk from her spinneret to throw at the flying wood sprite. It was the one position that exposed her vulnerability. While the armored shell was solid under the spider's front body section, the underside of the big round abdomen had only leathery skin. It had to move and flex so the spider could breathe.

Liliana ducked under and stabbed deep through that leathery skin, then sliced with her arm blade along one side of the spider's belly. Pete sunk the claws of both hands into spider flesh and ripped the spider open with brute force on the other side.

The stench of sewer and something cloyingly acidic like vomit hit the back of Liliana's throat and made her gag. Lady Daphne's guts spilled on the tile with a generous helping of slimy ichor and the viscous pearly white liquid that becomes silk when exposed to air.

Lady Daphne's shrieks reached a deafening crescendo. She leaped away from them while Liliana's blade was still buried in her body, ripping the deep gash open even wider and nearly yanking Liliana's arm out of its socket. Entrails dragged behind the giant spider and tangled in her legs as her limbs scrambled nonsensically in every direction.

Liliana could no longer move fast enough to get out of the way when one of those giant spider legs flailed in her direction. It knocked her across the balcony into the iron railing with no more control of her body than a rag doll flung by a child. The back of her head slammed into an iron support.

CHAPTER 16

SICK DAY

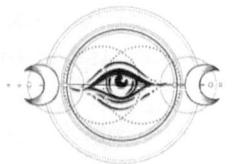

WHEN LILIANA WOKE UP, SHE WAS CLEAN AND IN HER own bed. The tick, tick, ticking of her many clocks sounded exactly as they should. Nothing could be too terribly wrong in the world as long as her clocks kept ticking along.

She wondered idly who had bathed her. Her left arm rested in a sling with lots of gauze to pad her injured shoulder. All her injuries had been bandaged and the glass chunks removed, but she didn't feel the itchiness of stitches. If she had been taken to a hospital, they would have put stitches in her skin that she would have to cut out before her fast-healing skin absorbed them. She had been well cared for by someone who was familiar with spider-kin needs. She suspected Doctor Nudd.

The only thing that hurt was her head.

She touched the back of her head gently and found an impressive goose egg.

Ow.

Beside her, on her little nightstand, next to a stained-glass lamp shaped like a tulip that she had found in a garage sale forty years ago, waited a note and a small bottle of white powder. The label on the bottle read, "Amphidosone." Liliana had been given amphidosone before. It was made from skin secretions of a frog-kin species, was highly addictive, and as "sopor" was sold on the street as a recreational drug. Taken in reasonable amounts, it proved an excellent analgesic for both Fae and beast-kin like her.

The note said, "Half a teaspoon dissolved in liquid for pain, as needed, at least four hours apart." Signed illegibly, the scrawl appeared short and had a capital N at the beginning. Doctor Nudd it was.

Rolling to a sitting position, she groaned. The only reason none of her injuries hurt before was because she hadn't moved. Now, everything hurt. She looked longingly at the white powder. In addition to dulling the pain, though, it would affect her like several shots of tequila affected a human. She had things to do before she could impair herself to that extent.

Her clocks said 7:20, and the sunshine coming through her brightly colored curtains said morning. She had appointments today. But she couldn't remember exactly when the first one would be. Her pounding head made thinking difficult.

Very slowly and gingerly, wearing a moss-green nightgown someone had dressed her in from of one of her own drawers, her feet bare, she walked to the room housing her business.

One of the shelves in her former dining room did not hold arcane knickknacks or clocks. It held big faux leather-bound books and an old-fashioned telephone with a handset connected to it by a curly wire. She replaced the old rotary phone late in the previous century when it became difficult to call many places without the tones push-button phones made. She had seen no reason to replace it since then, even though some people now considered voice-only wired phones to be antiques.

So she would not have to stay on her feet, she picked up the base and carried it to the table. The long cord trailed behind her.

Liliana lifted the largest book off the shelf with her one usable arm and considerable difficulty. She stifled a whimper. There were excellent reasons for the bandages along her ribs.

Pushing the crystal ball off-center, she set the big book on the round table. She would have to put that back later. The book with tabs on the side with the letters of the alphabet on them wasn't as heavy as the appointment book, thank goodness.

Ah. She had four appointments today, the first at 9:30 AM. She opened the book to the appropriate page to get the contact information for her first client and sat down carefully to avoid jarring her injuries. People might look down on her for using paper to keep track of contact information, but it could never be hacked and it was never "down," unlike the more modern ways of storing customer data.

One by one, she called all four of her clients for the day in the order of their appointments and either left a message or spoke to them, canceling or rescheduling. She considered also calling the clients she had scheduled for tomorrow, but decided not to. It was bad for business to cancel appointments, and hopefully, she would be feeling better by then.

Liliana lifted the huge appointment book and the smaller address book with difficulty and put them back on the shelf. She started to put the phone back but stopped. She picked up the receiver and dialed a number from memory. The phone rang twice.

"Willoughby residence," a cheerful voice answered.

"Hello, Mrs. Willoughby. You asked to schedule an appointment for next week. I can do that now."

"Madame Anna! I'm so glad to hear from you. I was worried sick. You seemed so upset when I left yesterday."

The rabbit-kin's comments warmed her. Liliana hadn't known anyone worried about her. "I am fine."

"That's wonderful to hear. Could I come in today then?"

"I am not that fine."

"Oh no. Are you hurt? Are you sick? Was it that red wolf? You said he wasn't dangerous, and Ben, Mr. Harper I mean, my boy Sam's teacher, he said that his Pete was a really good man. He doesn't know that he's a wolf-kin though, right? Of course he doesn't, him being a Normal and all. But in any case, you said the red wolf might die, and he didn't come home last night, and now Ben's real worried. I'm not worried, of course, not about a Celtic werewolf of all people, but I thought I'd ask anyway. For Ben. I wouldn't want him to worry unnecessarily after all."

Liliana started to answer, but Janice Willoughby did not seem to have much of a need to breathe.

"Ben's such a sweet man, and a wonderful teacher, Sam's favorite. I'd hate to see him get hurt. He loved the cookies and the cake I baked, and we really hit it off. It would be a crying shame if anything happened to his young man."

In a single day, Liliana marveled at how Pete had transformed from an evil werewolf beast who might eat Janice's children to the wolf-kin beloved of her son's favorite teacher.

To make certain that Pete was all right, Liliana opened her fourth eyes for a moment. He, too, was clean, bandaged, and in bed. The bed was huge, big enough for a half-dozen people to sleep in at once, and had an open window beside it with sheer blowing curtains.

Oh. Doctor Nudd's house.

She closed her fourth eyes quickly. The extra vision made her dizzy and nauseous.

It took her a few seconds to realize that Janice had stopped talking.

"Pete is fine. He did not die, but his thigh is injured. He stayed the night at a friend's house. He is still sleeping."

"Oh, that's so good to hear. I'm so glad. Ben will be completely relieved. Unless the friend was more than a friend, if you know what I mean. Then he probably wouldn't be so much. But I'm sure that his boyfriend wouldn't cheat on him like that. Ben's not the kind of man to put up with that sort of nonsense. I would sure hope that red wolf knew better than to do something like that to him. He's such a lovely man, you know?"

Liliana hesitated a moment to make sure Janice actually had stopped. "I have not yet met Ben Harper. Pete is very honorable. Pete was helping Sergeant Giovanni on a case last night in Raleigh, not cheating on his boyfriend."

"A case, huh? Those women who murdered the missing

soldiers? I saw on the news this morning that the Fort Liberty CID working with Fayetteville and Raleigh police caught them, but they were killed in some sort of firefight on the roof. I don't suppose you helped on that case too? Is that why Pete didn't die and you're not so fine this morning?"

The spider seer blinked. Janice Willoughby sometimes gave the impression with her rapid-fire speech and high energy levels that she lacked intelligence. Liliana knew that impression was false, but Janice's quick wit still surprised her now and again. "I made sure that Pete would not die before your husband needs him."

"That's...that's just..." Janice swallowed loud enough that Liliana could hear it over the phone.

Normally, Liliana looked at people with her fourth eyes while she talked to them on her phone, but right now, her head hurt too much to open any more eyes. All she really wanted to do was close the two she had open.

"Thank you," Janice said softly. "I, um, I just, thank you."

Janice's gratitude made Liliana uncomfortable. She had not saved Pete to help the Willoughbys. "Pete is my friend. I would not let him die if I could do anything to prevent it."

"Of course you wouldn't. He's lucky to have a friend like you."

"I am lucky to have a friend like him."

Janice chuckled. "And I thought he was dangerous."

"He is very dangerous." Liliana had watched the red wolf rip a widow spider's belly open with his bare hands last night.

Janice laughed outright. "Well, you know what I mean."

Liliana did not know what she meant, but decided her best bet to get off the phone any time soon was not to ask. "I have an opening for an appointment day after tomorrow sometime between 10 AM and 2 PM. Will that work for you?"

"Sure, Madame Anna. Put me down for noon."

"Done. Goodbye." Liliana hung up. She had to pull the big book back out to write down the new appointment.

When the book was safely back on its shelf, she mixed some of the white powder with a tall glass of cool water and went back to bed.

She had only just barely survived saving Pete's life once. Later, when her wounds were fully healed, she would have to find a way to help Pete avoid the other death she had foreseen when he protected Lou Willoughby.

Before that, there was something else she needed to do.

But not today.

It was her last thought before the medicine took her into a blessedly pain-free sleep.

CHAPTER 17

THE PRINCE AND THE OLD OAK

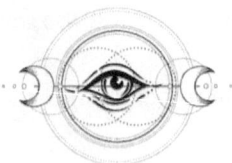

NEAR MIDNIGHT AFTER ANOTHER DAY THAT LILIANA HAD
been forced to reschedule appointments by her inability to open her
fourth eyes without dizziness and pain, Liliana crouched
uncomfortably on top of a streetlight in front of Janice
Willoughby's house, holding her injured arm close. In her good
hand, she held a line of her fine silk that ran to the ground and
ended in a loop strategically placed, nearly invisible in the stark light
and shadow beneath the streetlight.

Her injuries caused her constant irritation, especially the
headache and the shoulder, which ached just from the weight of her
arm. It should be in a sling, but she didn't want her weakness to be
visible tonight. The healing stab wound in her side itched
maddeningly. The gash on her face had sealed shut at least,
although one of her first and third eyes were partially swollen shut
from it.

The light shining down from the streetlight made her
imperceptible to the tall prince and the curly-haired wolf-kin with
the embossed leather collar. They would have to stare into the light
to see her, and she remained as motionless as the pole so as not to
draw their attention.

She felt through the pole the gut-level vibration as the Fae colonel called the Wolfhound to him with a Latin command steeped in earth magic.

She watched curiously, with her first, second, and third eyes as he transformed into his tall, elegant demi-stone form, like something a master sculptor created from a giant dark jewel. The side of his face looked as if some idiot tried to sand his skin with a stone file the roughness of a cheese grater, leaving ugly, sharp-edged imperfections in the otherwise glass-smooth surface. The shifting shadows that wreathed the Fae as he spoke to the Wolfhound weren't truly black as they had seemed in her earlier vision. Watching up this close, her second and third pair of eyes both recognized pure earth power. The Green in its darkest midnight shade, unseelie Green.

Watching the scene play out in front of her in reality, rather than in future possibility, the dark beauty of the man wreathed in earth power dazzled her enough that she almost missed the moment she should act.

As the Wolfhound on the sidewalk licked blood off his mouth, his canine face twisting from shock to snarling rage, Liliana flipped her line slightly to get the end to come up, then yanked the loop tight around the werewolf's ankle.

When the wolf-kin leapt toward the startled obsidian prince's throat, his outstretched claws stopped inches from polished stone skin. He yelped as he fell, stretched out facedown to the earth at the prince's feet.

Despite his surprise, Colonel Bennet wasted no time planting a boot on the back of the Wolfhound's neck to hold him down. He waved his hand, and the roots of the great oak writhed up, grabbing the frantically fighting werewolf.

The Sidhe prince stepped back to let the roots of the old oak tree have better access.

When the werewolf opened his mouth to scream, a root went into his open mouth, muffling the sound. It continued through and came out the back of the still feebly struggling wolf-kin's neck. Blood soaked into the earth and vanished.

In a few seconds, the werewolf was gone, the Willoughbys' lawn grew green and lush, and the old oak settled back to providing a sturdy anchor for the Willoughby children's tire swing.

The Fae prince leaned casually against the trunk, but Liliana could see the tremble in his free hand.

It had been a display of incredible power, but not an easy one. Colonel Bennet no doubt sought to hide weakness, since he had no idea who aided him or what they might want from him in return.

Liliana's third eyes were very nearsighted. They couldn't really see much of his mind or soul aura at this distance, especially not with the potent writhing aura of pure dark Green still playing around his legs. The earth's soul shone deep and powerful enough to dwarf any other, more subtle colors, like the sun hiding stars.

Liliana dropped gratefully from her uncomfortable perch on top of the streetlight, surreptitiously holding her elbow with her other hand until her legs bent to absorb the shock. It still hurt, but hopefully, her weakness didn't show. She stepped into the circle of light but stayed warily on the concrete sidewalk. He probably could not bring the old tree to life again tonight, but she wasn't taking any chances.

He nodded to her, a half-bow with a pained expression and a flash of red anger glowing in his eyes. "Thank you. Your intervention probably saved my life."

"You expected the Wolfhound who served your family to submit, not attack. He surprised you. You wouldn't have had time to defend yourself."

He waved a large hand, carved from a dark, living translucent jewel, an echo of the deep Green shimmering under the surface as if the earth's soul flowed within him. "And you aided me, even though you're already injured, I see." The last was said in a tone of exasperated irritation.

Liliana put a hand to the gash on her cheek self-consciously. She could hide her more severe injuries, but that one was obvious to anyone looking. "The assassin chose tonight to attack. I did not have the option to help on a night when I wasn't injured."

He huffed a chuckle. "I suppose not." The red glow of anger didn't fade. The Fae had rules about that sort of thing. The very strict, codified, black-and-white rules were far easier for the spider-kin to follow than the nebulous, often contradictory rules of social interaction among other races. It was very simple. If she saved his life, especially if it was difficult and cost her pain, he owed her a favor. By thanking her, no matter how much it angered him, he did the honorable thing and acknowledged the debt.

She could ask almost anything of him now.

But she hadn't done it to get anything from him like a lesser Fae would, or to one up him like another Sidhe would. "I needed the assassin stopped. I couldn't kill the Wolfhound with the defensive magic in his collar. You could." She gave him back the same head nod and half-bow, minus the anger. "Thank you for that."

Surprise shot the sharp ridges over his eyes that took the place of eyebrows up high, and the red glow of anger in his eyes vanished. By thanking him back, she negated his debt. Obsidian shoulders dropped an inch, releasing tension in muscles made of living stone. "That is generous of you." He couldn't thank her again, but the words were the Fae equivalent, turning gratitude into flattery, without implying debt.

She bowed to accept the compliment.

"I had hoped to speak to him," he commented with mild regret. "I'd like to know who sent him, and why."

"Your sister, Aurore, sent him to kill Pete."

"Ah," he said. "I suspected as much." He looked at her curiously. He did not try to get closer this time, still leaning against the tree. In addition to giving him time to recover, he also let her keep the distance she'd chosen between them. She appreciated the courtesy, and the indication she wouldn't have to fight him tonight. She was not in any shape to fight anyone. Neither, probably, was he after his expenditure of magical energy. "Last time I saw you, you told me you were going to kill Pete yourself if I didn't call him off. Did you get those injuries from fighting Pete?" He gestured to the gash on her cheek.

"I was not injured when I fought Pete, other than my feet got very cold and a little scraped, and one of Siobhan's bullets grazed my arm a little. He wasn't injured either, aside from a few bruises and a small bite. I got these wounds fighting at Pete's side. I convinced him I did not murder your soldiers. But when I told him he should talk to Lady Daphne, the widow spider, I didn't know she was protecting the real murderer. I was injured fighting widow spiders at his side."

"He never mentioned that in any of his reports. But I did notice some suspiciously glossed-over aspects, and I saw you on some video surveillance footage we confiscated. Pete is usually better about telling me everything."

"I asked him not to mention me in anything official. I prefer that the government doesn't know I exist. He respected my request." After a moment, she added, "I like Pete."

The startled, barely there smile on the obsidian face with the silver needle teeth should have been cold, even frightening. All the expressions she'd seen on that stone face up to now had been. Instead, the tiny curve of polished stone lips was a flash of warmth and humor that had Liliana smiling back. "I like Pete too," the obsidian prince with the crown of silver horns said, his melodious deep voice amused.

"Can you please leave me out of the official reports also? My species is nearly extinct because when officials know we exist, they keep killing us."

The tall, crowned prince looked down at the place where the assassin that nearly killed him vanished under the earth. "I will honor your wish in this. Pete's report already doesn't mention you. I'll make sure the footage that includes you gets accidentally erased."

Liliana knew better than to thank a Fae. "That is very generous of you," she said, with feeling, and smiled up at him. She did not feel safe enough yet to step onto a living lawn with the powerful Fae, but she wished he would come closer.

They stood there smiling at each other for a few seconds, and his tiny warm smile broadened. "Do you happen to know why my sister sent an assassin to kill Pete?" the Fae colonel asked her.

"Yes, I know." Liliana wasn't sure if she should tell him. Aurore wanted Pete's enchanted sword enough to send an assassin to kill him for it. She didn't want Pete's powerful protector to feel the same desire.

The prince sighed, his smile vanishing. Another Fae would bargain with him for the information.

She hated the way the idea of bargaining for information sucked every trace of joy out of his face, making it hard and cold again. As he opened his mouth, no doubt to ask her what she wanted in exchange for the answer to his question, she blurted out, "He has a sword." *So much for deciding if he should know or not.* "Aurore Principessa wants it. The Wolfhound was meant to kill him and his human beloved and steal it."

Colonel Bennet's face of living stone shifted smoothly like oily black liquid, first to a flash of startled pleasure, then to a puzzled expression. "Why would she send an assassin to this continent to kill Pete and steal his sword?"

Liliana shrugged. "The assassin didn't know. Neither do I."

He nodded, the silver crown that was part of his head making the motion more pronounced and regal like the movements of a noble stag. Then he shifted.

His body shrank to a size that was merely tall rather than giant. A face of soft, deep brown flesh replaced hard black stone. The silver horn crown shrank into his skull and vanished, replaced by a buzz of coarse black hair with a streak of white on one side.

He took a deep breath and stood straight, dropping the hand from the tree trunk that had been holding a lot of his weight. His hands still trembled a little, but he was beginning to recover.

She understood the rules of Fae bargaining and had done her best to sidestep them, but she also needed information. Since she had given him valuable information for free, maybe he would do the same. "The Wolfhounds serve your family, and their main purpose is as a defense against Celtic wolves. Why would you kill one to protect a red wolf?"

Colonel Bennet's human face went blank, looking more like a statue than his mobile demi-stone face had. "I did mention that I like Pete."

Liliana smiled wistfully at the smoke snake of power coiled around his right knee. It was truth, but not an answer to her question.

It was a lot to ask of a Fae prince to not act like a Fae prince.

She sighed, disappointed, and turned away from him. She had given away her only bargaining chips. If he wasn't willing to give her the information, she had nothing left to use to pay for it.

She walked down the concrete sidewalk back toward her house, holding up the elbow of her bad arm to ease the pain in her shoulder.

His voice behind her wasn't loud, but it carried to her clearly, vibrating with the depth of earth magic and the ring of a very precise oath. "I will not be bound by the factions and blood feuds of the Old World."

She turned to look behind her with a delighted smile, but the handsome Fae colonel was gone, a swirl of dark Green settled back into the lush grass where he had been.

Thank you for reading! Did you enjoy? Please add your review because nothing helps an author more and encourages readers to take a chance on a book than a review.

And don't miss the next book of the Liliana and the Fae of Fayetteville, EXPLOSIVE CHEMISTRY, available now. Turn the page for a sneak peek!

Also be sure to sign up for the City Owl Press newsletter to receive notice of all book releases!

SNEAK PEEK OF EXPLOSIVE CHEMISTRY

The bloody image of two young women in military uniform being shot in the back of the head jolted Liliana awake. She sat up abruptly, her heart pounding, a pointless "No!" forming on her lips.

Her fourth eyes that saw things in other times and places were already open, the source of the ugly dream.

Who are they?

But her mental question did not elicit any new visions, just a repeat of the same horrors. She needed more information to have any chance of saving the women. Her fourth vision showed her nothing near them but a forest, trees, and grass. There was a pine leaning on an oak tree, and a bush with lovely white flowers beneath it. The oak tree had no leaves, so it must have been winter. The plant life looked like the local forests, but that same kind of forest could be anywhere for hundreds of miles around. North Carolina had a lot of forests, especially since paper, and for the most part, wood, had become obsolete.

The two women both had faces in her vision that shimmered with Otherness. They were not Normal humans, but that was all Liliana could tell about them.

Death overwhelmed her fourth vision under the best of circumstances. When she slept, she didn't have as much control over her vision as she did when awake. She had no idea why the two women she didn't even know were suddenly in her mind, or if the vision was of the future or of the past. Oddly, it had a trace of the overbright reflections of the future mixed with the muted color tones of the past.

They can't die both in the past and in the future.

It made no sense.

She got up, feeling tired and achy, and determined not to let it stop her.

Liliana had taken a sick day after nearly being killed a couple days before. Much to her chagrin, she had been forced to take a second sick day by the inability to open her fourth eyes to see the past and future without waves of dizziness from her head injury. She could not get paid for her job as Madame Anna Sees All when she couldn't open the large swirly pair of spikder-kin eyes on her forehead to see anything.

The awful dream told the spider-kin seer one important thing: her fourth eyes were once again fully functional.

That meant she could get back to work. Which was good. She hadn't cancelled the appointments for the day, hoping that would be the case. Spider-kin healed fast and cancelling appointments was bad for business.

Liliana removed all the bandages and examined her injuries in the mirror. When she closed her six spider eyes, leaving only her first, human eyes open, her thick dark hair hid the tiny crinkles where they closed. The image in the mirror looked just like a petite young Normal. It was good camouflage. Normals outnumbered Others a hundred to one and tended toward violence when faced with "monsters." She nodded at the image. She could pass.

Her face and body still clearly showed that she'd been in a battle recently, though. The gash on her cheek looked particularly ugly. The wide, jagged slice made by a widow spider's spiked limb was closed but still a livid purple with mottled green and yellow old bruising over that side of her face. At least Doctor Nudd had taped the gash shut. That helped it heal more cleanly and quickly.

All of Liliana's small cuts from her and Pete's recent battle had healed to the point that only raised pink welts were visible. The swelling on the back of her head was much reduced. She could rotate her neck and open all eight of her eyes without her head feeling like it would fall off.

The only real pain was from her shoulder wound. She supported one arm with the other as she carefully tested how much she could move it. She closed all her eyes as a wave of sadness came with the pain of moving her arm. Stella, the widow spider, had stabbed clear through her shoulder, and Liliana had used that leverage on her limb to drag the brave warrior to her death over the side of a tall building.

Under other circumstances, she and Stella might have been friends. Liliana mourned the death of a fellow spider-kin doing what she must to protect her nest sisters. But if she had not killed Stella, the widow spider would have killed Liliana, so... She sighed. She killed only when she had to, as all three of her parents taught. As long as that was true, she would still find the image in the mirror acceptable, but that didn't mean she couldn't be sad about the necessity.

As she dressed, she cheered herself with thoughts of the people she'd met over the last few days. Doctor Peter Teague, a civilian bio scientist with the Criminal Investigation Division for Fort Liberty, and a deadly Celtic wolf-kin, accused her of murder and tried to kill her before becoming the closest friend she'd had in years. Siobhan, the little person and flower sprite who owned the custom weapons shop Emerald Arms, a few doors down from her own shop, had also tried to kill her. Then the sprite helped her and Pete survive their battle with the widow spiders, the real killers Pete mistook her for. The unseelie oak goblin, Doctor Nudd, had also tried to kill her, but he made up for that later by loaning her his homemade warm sweater and healing her injuries after the battle.

She had an odd way of meeting people lately.

On the plus side, she had been getting out more, and her life could no longer be described as either boring or lonely.

Opening her fourth eyes, the swirling opalescent lavender and teal ones set above her eyebrows, she took a quick look forward in time to check the weather like she did every morning. It would get chilly and rainy again later. Winter in Fayetteville tended to be sunshiny one day and cold and wet the next. She added cozy purple tights with her black leotard under her usual flowing, brightly colored, homemade skirt. She chose a blouse made of warm velvet scarves with wide, drapey sleeves like mini-wings that went all the way to the wrist. They would keep her arms warm without restricting the natural weaponry hidden in her forearms.

Her shoulder wound would take a week before she could go without a sling. She put the sling on her arm and frowned. The medical sling Doctor Nudd gave her was a plain, dull light blue canvas. It did not go well with the sapphire blue velvet top, and the skirt with glittery silver bead trim that complimented it.

Liliana took the sling off, chose a scarf from her chest of drawers, and tied it around her neck. She slipped her arm into it and looked in the mirror again.

The leafy-green, floral patterned silk scarf held her arm without pulling on her sore shoulder, and it looked much nicer than the plain canvas one. She nodded with satisfaction and walked into the converted dining room that served as her place of business, Madame Anna Sees All. She closed the door that led to the rest of her house and checked that the crystal ball was where it belonged, in the exact center of the round table in the middle of the room.

She had scheduled multiple appointments back-to-back, far more than she normally would in a day, to catch up. The first knock on the business door came only minutes later. She welcomed the pair of young wood nymphs who entered in a cloud of giggles and lilac perfume.

Bowing, she waved her arms to gesture them in, and chanted, "Madame Anna sees all. Pay me what you feel is fair for truth that cannot be seen by other eyes. I see what is, what has been, and what might be. Ask and the truth shall be yours."

Her first appointments went reasonably well. Everyone insisted on asking what had happened to her shoulder and her face. The gash on her cheek from Stella's last attack was the first thing everyone noticed. It didn't particularly bother Liliana until they mentioned it, unlike her shoulder injury that restricted her movements, or the persistent itch from the gash on her ribs.

When she answered, "I was stabbed by a giant spider," the nymph girls laughed as if she made a joke, even though they were Others. They knew that such things could exist.

Her second client, a Normal human who probably didn't know such things existed, rolled his eyes and said, "That's a good story. You'll have a hard time topping it later."

When her best client, Janice Willoughby, a rabbit-kin homemaker, came in, she took one look at Liliana, covered her mouth with her hand, and interrupted Liliana's usual client welcome speech to say, "What happened?"

"I was stabbed by a giant spider helping Pete on that case a few days ago. I am fine, though. The injuries are already healing."

"Oh, Madame Anna, you could have been killed. I heard on the news about the serial killers in Raleigh targeting soldiers from Fort Liberty. They weren't Normals, were they? What were they really?"

"A nest of widow spiders." Liliana shrugged. She looked at the shoulder strap of her client's purse, a soft-looking blue denim material with appliqued flowers. Liliana wondered if it was Janice's own handiwork.

Janice gasped and her face blanched. "A whole nest of them! I'd scream and run if I saw even one. It's a wonder you weren't killed."

"I did not die," Liliana reassured her favorite client. "The widow spiders died. I am fine."

Janice insisted that Liliana tell her the full story. As talkative as Janice was, Liliana also found her to be an excellent listener. The spider-kin felt an odd relief after she shared the story of Pete, the red wolf-kin, hunting her, how she defeated him in single combat, and later risked her life to save him and his friend, Sergeant Zoe Giovanni. It was as if she had been holding something heavy all by herself, and now Janice Willoughby held one end of it for her.

Apparently, having someone she could talk to honestly about her life was soothing in some way. She had noticed this with her clients—that they would often pay the spider seer to simply listen to them talk about their lives when they had no real questions to ask. That had always seemed odd to her. Now she understood.

Long after her appointment ended, Janice stayed and talked with Liliana. When Liliana started to feel hungry, she did something she had not done in a very long time. She invited Janice Willoughby into her home to share lunch.

After telling the rabbit-kin about the recent events in her life, Liliana had little else to say, but Janice didn't have any trouble filling up the silence. While they ate grilled cheese sandwiches and drank tea, she kept chatting amiably about her children and her husband, Lou. She also spoke about rapidly becoming close friends with Ben Harper, Pete's Normal boyfriend who was one of Janice's son's teachers.

Liliana was surprised to find that having her best client in her home did not bother her like she'd assumed it would. She enjoyed having the cheerful rabbit-kin sharing her personal space.

In fact, she thought perhaps, once she was fully healed, she should go out on a social visit herself, her first in decades. The thought made her stomach a little queasy with nerves, but Liliana was not a coward. She had promised Doctor Nudd she would return his sweater. She would not let fear stop her from keeping her word to the kind goblin.

In addition, having seen him fight twice now, it was clear to Liliana that Pete needed more training. He had all the raw materials of a great warrior—courage without bounds, an indomitable will, intelligence, and incredible levels of brute power—but he did not know how to use those strengths to best advantage. Beyond training, he needed two other things to survive the attack she'd foreseen from a pack of assassins from the Order of the Wolfhound: something to defeat the protective magic of the crown collars the Wolfhounds wore, and allies.

Liliana picked up their plates and went to her kitchen to fetch more tea for herself and Janice.

Pete would be dead already without his allies. Colonel Bennet, who secretly watched over Pete, was even more secretly an unseelie Fae prince. He was also the only reason the first Wolfhound assassin who came to Fayetteville had not already slain Pete. Well, the Colonel's abilities plus a little help from Liliana.

The only reason she and Pete had survived their encounter with the widow spiders was the timely aid of Siobhan and her machine gun. The value of good allies was incalculable.

Doctor Nudd, in particular, would be essential to Pete's survival. If an eight-foot oak goblin stood with Pete when he fought, that would certainly improve his chances. Not to mention the doctor's healing abilities after the battle.

Liliana opened her fourth eyes and looked along the goblin's life path.

How can I make sure Doctor Nudd will be there to help when Pete faces the Wolfhounds?

She saw the gentle doctor pierced with a sword, blood bubbling from his lips as he died. The power and clarity of the image meant that it would happen soon and was nearly certain.

Oh.

The tea tray in Liliana's hands tilted without her noticing, spilling tea and cups all over her woven carpet.

Oh.

Janice jumped up from the chair and grabbed the tray from her hands. "What is it, Madame Anna? What did you see?"

Janice set the tray on the coffee table and gently guided the spider seer to the couch by one elbow.

Liliana would have missed the couch in her distraction without the help. "Doctor Nudd is going to be murdered."

"Oh! That's awful." Janice picked up the mostly unbroken tea cups off the carpet. "He's the nice goblin who fixed up your injuries, right?"

Liliana nodded. "He is also Pete's closest friend and mentor. Pete will die if Doctor Nudd is not there to fight beside him the next time he is attacked. And he will mourn if Doctor Nudd dies." After a moment, she added, "I will mourn too."

"Is that why he's going to be murdered, do you think? Because he's friends with the Celtic werewolf? There's a lot of Others who have a hate on for Pete's kind."

"It is possible. Let me look." With a feeling of dread, she opened her fourth eyes again to look into the life path of Pete and his other allies.

Sergeant Giovanni had narrowly avoided one death at the hands of the widow spiders, only to walk blithely toward another. "Sergeant Giovanni, who is also Pete's friend, has at least three possible deaths waiting for her, one very soon. In two weeks."

Colonel Bennet, the handsome Fae prince who had killed a Wolfhound to protect Pete would be dead in less than a year. His entire identity was wrapped in secrets, so Liliana didn't say anything about him out loud. Seeing him die sent a jerk to her belly that made her fight not to throw up her lunch.

She swallowed, then said, "Detective Jackson will die within days, the same time as Sergeant Giovanni. Or Pete might die trying to protect her from an Other killer." Detective Jackson had been with Sergeant Giovanni and Pete when they accused Liliana of murder, but she refused to believe Liliana was guilty with no evidence other than Liliana being spider-kin. The detective had been the only one who believed in Liliana's innocence.

Janice sat down on the coffee table facing Liliana. "Wow. That's a lot of murder all of a sudden."

So much death.

Liliana shuddered and wrapped her arms around herself. "I have not seen so many images of people dying all at once since I lost two of my three parents, two brothers, one sister, and all their families in the same year. And that was when Nazis were killing everyone."

"These are all the red wolf's friends, though. You know werewolves are trouble, and Celtic wolves even more than most. I hope Ben is safe."

A quick glance showed no near danger to Ben Harper, the Normal teacher who owned Pete's heart. "Ben is not involved in most of what I see. He should be all right." Although, he would have died, too, if she and Colonel Bennet hadn't already slain the first Wolfhound.

Janice bit her lip. "Are you in any danger yourself?"

Even knowing that it was a question she probably did not want to see the answer to, Liliana looked into her future. She saw a dozen different deaths. Each vision was flickery like a candle flame in the wind, shifting with uncertainty, but they all involved Pete in one way or another. "Yes, the more I am involved in Pete's life, the more ways I might die."

She closed all her eyes, overwhelmed. Clearly, becoming Pete's ally had a detrimental effect on one's life expectancy.

"Madame Anna, I know you've always been the one to give me advice, but it sounds like being Pete's friend is really dangerous. He doesn't think you're a killer anymore, so he shouldn't bother you." Janice patted her knee. "Maybe you'd be better off just going back to the way things were?"

Liliana considered Janice's advice. If the spider seer went back to her old life, to watching the future of Others, guiding them safely around obstacles, and staying out of the larger affairs of the Other community in North Carolina, she would probably live a lot longer.

"Pete and all my new friends would die." Her life would go back to being routine, boring, and lonely. "I do not want to be alone anymore."

Janice squeezed her knee and nodded. "I didn't even think about how lonely you must get never talking to anyone who doesn't pay you."

"I am also unwilling to be the kind of person who sees danger to my friends coming and does nothing." Even if it meant increasing her probability of meeting an untimely end. That was not the child her three brave warrior parents raised. That was not the woman she wanted to see in the mirror. "Also, Pete trusts me."

To her surprise, Liliana concluded that being worthy of that trust was more important to her than anything else, including increasing the likelihood of her survival.

Janice nodded and sat back. "I respect that. Okay, then. Is there anything you can do to help?"

Having saved Pete from the certain death she'd seen a few days before, Liliana felt confident that she *could* change the dark futures she saw, although it might cost her own life. "Changing fate is always dangerous. I must be careful, or I could make things even worse."

"Worse, how?" Janice asked. "Could something happen to other people?"

That was a disturbing thought. "Other people may already be in danger." Liliana had spent decades keeping her clients safe and guiding them toward happiness. Her clients made up a fair percentage of the Others in Fayetteville, and even a small percentage of the Normal humans. "I only looked at my friends' futures."

Is this tide of death focused, or will it harm more people I watch over as well?

Her fourth eyes showed her an ugly chain reaction, pushing outward like ripples spreading in a lake of blood. "Oh."

"What is it, Madame Anna?" Janice bit the cuticle on her thumb.

"If Doctor Nudd dies, then Pete dies, then Sergeant Giovanni and Detective Jackson die, then everyone those two police women, military and civilian, might have protected dies or has awful things happen to them with no one to stop it. This could be devastating to all of Fayetteville." The fate of her entire community was tangled with the fate of her friends.

"Where is all this coming from all of a sudden?" Janice got up and paced back and forth in Liliana's small living room. "You and Ben's man, Pete, stopped the ones who were killing those soldiers. That should have made us all safer."

Janice was right. Wiping out the widow spiders should have stopped the red tide of violent death, not made the situation worse.

Why is everyone still in so much danger? What did we miss?

Another quick flash of the two military women being executed from behind made her shiver. They must be key in some way.

How are they related? Why do I keep seeing them?

Her fourth eyes failed to see an answer. The deaths themselves clouded and overwhelmed everything else. As always. "I keep seeing these two women being killed. They're soldiers in uniform. Others of some kind. I don't understand how, but they're related to the source of the danger in some way."

Janice sat next to her on the couch. "Well, whatever you decide to do, Madame Anna, you watch your back. Those widow spiders hurt you pretty bad. Whatever is coming sounds like it's a lot worse."

Despite the lingering horror all the visions of death left her with, she smiled. "I will be careful." Janice Willoughby worried about her. It was nice that someone did.

Clocks chimed, telling Liliana it was almost time for her next appointment. She had to ask Janice to leave. She found that she did not want the rabbit-kin to go.

"I'll see you next week then, at the regular time," Janice said.

Liliana nodded, said, "Goodbye," as social rules required, and started to shut the door.

"Um, Madame Anna?" Janice said.

"Yes?"

"I'm glad you're okay. You be real careful helping your friends, and...I really enjoyed lunch."

Liliana smiled at Janice's tennis shoes. "I did too."

After she shut the door, Liliana considered the Fae Colonel, wondering if he could be the source of so much danger. Having a Sidhe with the potential to bond with the land on this side of the ocean was something she'd feared since she was smuggled into this country. The land always chose Sidhe Fae as rulers. So as long as there were no Sidhe royalty on this continent, all the Others who had fled here were safe. No non-native Fae had bonded with this land in over two-hundred years, and most of the native Fae had been killed or driven into hiding.

If the Colonel did manage to bond to the land and another

Sidhe Fae opposed him, like his sister Aurore Principessa, who was known for her cruelty...

It was a recipe for war.

Maybe he is the source of the rising tide of death.

Letting the Colonel's fated death happen without interfering might be best for everyone.

But he is handsome.

The thought came unbidden and was supremely unhelpful in her attempts to find a logical way through the morass of death and intertwined fates.

But he *was* handsome, from his shimmering obsidian demi-stone form to the high cheekbones, full lips, and intense gaze of his human form. Regardless of her attraction to him, she could not condemn a man to death without knowing more about him. After all, he had protected both Pete and Sergeant Giovanni. Plus, he was strong and fierce, and had a smooth, deep voice that made her belly warm. While it might be wiser to do nothing and let his death find him, she would not find that at all easy.

The right kind of Fae ruler had, historically, caused the land to flourish and ushered in golden ages of plenty and peace. Arthur Pendragon had only been half Sidhe and therefore mortal. Yet his brief rule was still remembered.

Baba Yaga, on the other hand, blasted her own land to win a war. Countless died, both millions of Normal and thousands of Others. It took a century for the land to recover. Baba Yaga was gone now. The Green, the power and soul of the earth, did not take kindly to those who betrayed it.

Liliana did not know what sort of man this Fae prince was or what his ambitions might be. But he had nearly a year to live. Later, Liliana would decide if she should try to save the Fae prince.

First, she would have to save Sergeant Giovanni. Again. And Detective Jackson, and possibly Pete as well. And then Doctor Nudd.

A knock on her business door let her know that her next client had arrived, a nice seelie Fae sylph. His wife was a soldier deployed overseas, and he worried constantly.

After work, she would explore future paths to find a way to change her favorite people's dark fates.

* * *

Don't stop now. Keep reading with your copy of EXPLOSIVE CHEMISTRY

Don't miss the book two in the Liliana and the Fae of Fayetteville series, EXPLOSIVE CHEMISTRY, available now, and find more from Paige E. Ewing at www.paigeewing.com

As a spider-kin seer, Liliana's eyes can see the future. What she didn't see was her visions leading her out of her voluntary seclusion and into the lives of the first friends she's had in decades. Friends Liliana just rescued from the deadly venom of widow spiders.

Determined to keep the warmth of belonging and stay out of her shell, she looks into the future again and sees death. Her friends Pete the red wolf, Siobhan the fairy sprite, and Nudd the goblin doctor will all die soon—if she doesn't take steps to nudge the future and discover who was behind the widow spiders.

Except saving her friends will tie Liliana even closer to the handsome and dangerous Unseelie prince Colonel Bennett, and her heart may not come out of that battle unscathed.

Please sign up for the City Owl Press newsletter for chances to win special subscriber-only contests and giveaways as well as receiving information on upcoming releases and special excerpts.

All reviews are **welcome** and **appreciated**. Please consider leaving one on your favorite social media and book buying sites.

For books in the world of romance and speculative fiction that embody Innovation, Creativity, and Affordability, check out City Owl Press at www.cityowlpress.com.

Acknowledgments

This book took a lot of years, a lot of rewrites, and a lot of feedback to come to fruition. I've had so much support and help all along, starting with LittleBounce and D Squirrel way back in the day, that I can't possibly name everyone.

Thanks to my crit groups from Slug Tribe to Shlomi, Jim, Mike, Tom, Victor, Iolo, Gryphon, and Sheri of White Gold Wielders (WGW). I'm a far better writer for having let you all tear apart my words and point at the flaws.

And thanks to nanowrimo in general, and the Texas Elsewhere nano group in particular for keeping me always drafting new things.

Alden, Tex, Jen, Nomolosk, and Robo are the best for poking me to do some twenty minute writing sprints every evening, so I never feel like I'm writing alone. Positive peer pressure for the win.

Thanks to my agent, Michelle Hauck for believing in me and my work, and my City Owl editor Lisa Green for challenging me to take it to another level.

And thanks most of all to my long suffering husband Joe, who put up with me ignoring him for many, many hours while I typed away on a keyboard.

About the Author

PAIGE E. EWING writes about superheroes and sentient cities, were-spiders and gun-loving fairies, werewolves and fighter pilots. For her day job, she gives speeches and writes about big data analysis and data architectures, a subject which also doubles as a sleep aid for many.

For fun, she shoots arrows, and throws axes. She lives in the middle of nowhere, Texas, and will show you far too many pictures of her garden if you let her. She once invented a way to grow food on Mars that NASA liked, and has a cute trophy to show for it. Her dogs and horses are unimpressed.

www.paigeewing.com

 x.com/PaigeEwing

 mastodon.social/@PaigeEwing

 instagram.com/paigeewing_author

ABOUT THE PUBLISHER

City Owl Press is a cutting edge indie publishing company, bringing the world of romance and speculative fiction to discerning readers.

Escape Your World. Get Lost in Ours!

www.cityowlpress.com

facebook.com/YourCityOwlPress
x.com/cityowlpress
instagram.com/cityowlbooks
pinterest.com/cityowlpress

www.ingramcontent.com/pod-product-compliance
Lightning Source LLC
Chambersburg PA
CBHW020322260626
47156CB00004B/1334